A Merry LITTLE VENDETTA

Kathleen Kelly
USA Today Bestselling Author

A Merry Little Vendetta

Kathleen Kelly
USA Today Bestselling Author

All efforts have been made to ensure the correct grammar and punctuation in the book. If you do find any errors, please e-mail Kathleen Kelly: kathleenkellyauthor@gmail.com
Thank you.

Disclaimer: The material in this book contains graphic language and sexual content and is intended for mature audiences, ages 18 and older.

ISBN: 978-1922883230

Editing by Swish Design & Editing
Proofreading by Swish Design & Editing
Book design by Swish Design & Editing
Cover design by CT Cover Creations
Cover Image Copyright 2025
First Edition 2025

DEDICATION

For the women who've been underestimated.
May you always find your power and someone
who sees it.

For anyone who's ever guarded their heart.
This story is proof that even the most dangerous
men can learn to love gently.

Chapter 1

Alessandro

The scent of pine and cinnamon hits me before I even push through the door.

I pause on the threshold of Petals & Pines, my hand still on the frosted glass, and wonder, not for the first time today, what the hell I'm doing here. I don't buy flowers. My men buy flowers for me, usually for funerals I've caused, occasionally for mothers I'm obligated to appease. But here I am, Alessandro De Luca, standing outside a flower shop in the middle of downtown Seattle like some lovesick teenager instead of the man who controls half this city's underground.

The bell above the door chimes as I step inside, and I'm immediately assaulted by color.

Christ. So much color.

Everywhere I look, flowers and plants hang from

the ceiling in artful arrangements, climb up rustic wooden shelves, and spill out of vintage metal buckets. Deep red roses that remind me of blood. White lilies that make me think of funerals. Golden chrysanthemums catch the warm light from Edison bulbs strung across exposed brick walls. But it's the Christmas decorations that really catch my attention, including garlands of fresh pine wound with fairy lights, wreaths adorned with red berries and gold ribbon, and poinsettias in every shade from cream to crimson.

The shop itself is small, maybe thirty feet deep, but every inch is utilized. The walls are exposed brick on one side, painted a soft sage green on the other. Wooden crates serve as display stands, each one labeled with chalk script that's almost too pretty to read. There's a vintage ladder propped in the corner, draped with eucalyptus. A velvet settee, the color of moss, sits near the window, probably for customers who need to rest while their significant others agonize over bouquet choices.

And Christmas music plays softly from somewhere, not the obnoxious pop versions, but a jazzy rendition of "Have Yourself a Merry Little Christmas" that doesn't make me want to shoot the speakers.

It's warm, inviting, and the complete opposite of everywhere I usually spend my time.

Then I see *her*.

She's standing behind a worktable near the back, surrounded by a controlled chaos of stems and ribbons. Her dark hair is piled on top of her head in a messy knot, held in place by what appears to be a pencil. She's wearing a cream-colored sweater that's far too big for her, the sleeves pushed up to her elbows, and a green apron covered in smudges of dirt and plant matter. Her hands move with practiced efficiency as she trims the stem of a white rose at an angle, her bottom lip caught between her teeth in concentration.

She hasn't noticed me yet.

I take the opportunity to study her, the way I would any potential threat or asset. Except she's neither. She's just stunning, but not in the polished, high-maintenance way of the women who usually orbit my world. There's no designer anything on her, and no obvious effort to impress. A smudge of dirt crosses her cheekbone, and there's a small rip in the knee of her jeans. But when she finally glances up, and our eyes meet, I forget how to breathe.

Her eyes are the color of honey in sunlight—warm, golden brown with flecks of amber. They widen slightly as she takes me in, and I'm suddenly, uncomfortably aware of how I must look—perfectly tailored black wool coat, black suit beneath it, and black shoes polished to a mirror shine. The only color on me is the deep burgundy of my tie, and even that's muted. I know what I look like. I've cultivated this image carefully to be cold, controlled, and dangerous. The kind of man you cross the street to avoid.

But she doesn't look away.

Instead, she sets down her pruning shears, wipes her hands on her apron, and smiles.

It's not a nervous smile. Not a flirtatious one. It's just genuine and warm, like I'm any other customer who wandered in from the December cold.

"Hi there!" Her voice matches her smile. It's bright, friendly, with just a hint of rasp that does something unfortunate to my pulse. "Welcome to Petals & Pines. Are you looking for something specific or just browsing?"

I open my mouth. Close it. Open it again.

Marco, my second-in-command, would be laughing his ass off if he could see me right now. Alessandro De Luca, the man who's negotiated million-dollar deals and stared down the barrel of more guns than he can count, struck dumb by a woman in a flower shop.

"Flowers," I finally manage, then immediately want to kick myself. No shit, I'm in a flower shop.

But she doesn't laugh at me. Her smile gets a little bigger, revealing a dimple in her left cheek that should probably be illegal.

"Well, you've definitely come to the right place." She moves out from behind her worktable, and I notice she's shorter than I expected. Maybe five-foot-four in the worn boots she's wearing, and she is delicate, almost fragile-looking.

The thought of anyone putting their hands on her sends an immediate, irrational surge of protectiveness through me.

"Christmas flowers?" she asks, gesturing to the festive displays. "Or something else?"

"Christmas," I confirm, my voice rougher than usual, so I clear my throat. "For my mother."

It's not entirely a lie. I do need to send something to my mother in Naples. But that's not why I'm here.

I'm here because three days ago, I watched this woman from the coffee shop across the street, laughing with a customer while she wrapped their purchase, and I haven't been able to get her out of my head since. I'm here because I did something I never do, I asked questions and found out her name is Elena Harper. She opened this shop two years ago and lives in the apartment above it.

Also, she's single.

That last piece of information probably shouldn't have pleased me as much as it did.

"How wonderful!" She clasps her hands together, and I notice the silver rings on her fingers, one with a moonstone and another with what looks like a tiny, pressed flower under glass. "Is she traditional? Modern? What's her style?"

I think of my mother, who has presided over the

De Luca family's charitable foundation for the past thirty years while tactfully ignoring exactly where the money comes from. The woman who arranges white roses in crystal vases and attends mass every Sunday.

"Traditional," I say. "Elegant. Classic."

Elena nods thoughtfully, already moving toward a display of deep red roses. "These are gorgeous, obviously. Can't go wrong with roses at Christmas, but..." She pauses, tilting her head as she studies me. "I'm sensing these might be a little... expected? For your mother?"

I'm not sure what shows on my face, but something makes her grin.

"See, I knew it. She probably gets roses from everyone. Let me show you something special."

She leads me deeper into the shop, past buckets of what I think are carnations, little tiny white flowers, and tall stems of some purple ones I have no idea what it is. Her presence is like a living thing, all warmth, energy, and light.

She talks as she walks, her hands gesturing animatedly. "The thing about Christmas flowers is everyone defaults to red and white, right? Poinsettias, roses, lilies. And don't get me wrong, they're beautiful, but there's so much more you can do." She stops in front of a section I hadn't even noticed, tucked into a corner near the back. "Like this."

I look where she's pointing and actually catch my breath.

The arrangement she's indicating to is breathtaking. White blooms rise from a bed of dark greenery. There is pine, cedar, and something with silver-green leaves I don't recognize. Woven through it all are branches with small red berries, and the whole thing is accented with touches of gold-painted pinecones, subtle ribbon, and a dusting of something that catches the light like snow.

"Amaryllis flowers represent pride and beauty," Elena says softly, reverently, like she's sharing a secret. "But also determination and strength. The white ones specifically symbolize purity and innocence, which feels right for a mother. And I love them for Christmas because they're elegant without being obvious. This arrangement has all the classic Christmas elements, including pine, berries, and gold, but it's elevated. Sophisticated."

She looks up at me, those honey-colored eyes searching my face. "Does she sound like someone who would appreciate sophisticated?"

"Yes," I say, because my mother absolutely would. But also because I think I'd agree to anything right now if it meant Elena kept looking at me like that, like my opinion actually matters.

"Perfect!" She beams, and I feel it physically as warmth spreads through my chest. "I'll make this fresh for you. It'll take me about twenty minutes if you want to browse, or you can wait on the settee. I have hot cider if you'd like some?"

Hot cider in a flower shop with Christmas jazz playing in the background?

This is so far removed from my everyday existence. I might as well be on another planet.

"I'll wait," I hear myself say. "Thank you."

She gives me another one of those smiles that makes her whole face light up and practically bounces back to her worktable. I should sit on the settee as she suggested. Instead, I find myself drifting closer to where she's working, watching her hands as she selects stems with a critical eye.

"So..." she says without looking up, her tone conversational, "... first time at Petals & Pines?"

"Yes."

"Well, welcome. I'm Elena, the owner. And you are?"

I hesitate for a fraction of a second. In my world, names have power. Giving mine to a stranger is rarely wise, but something about the way she asks in a casual, friendly, no-hidden-agenda manner makes me want to tell her.

"Alessandro."

"Alessandro." She repeats it slowly, like she's tasting the syllables. Her pronunciation is perfect, with the proper Italian inflection. "That's a beautiful name. Italian?"

"Yes. My family is from Naples."

"No kidding? My grandparents are from Sicily. Russo is about as Italian as it gets." She grins at me over a white amaryllis bloom. "Small world."

Russo. The same surname as the family who's been trying to muscle into my territory for the past six months.

The family who made a move on one of my warehouses last week.

The family I'm currently at war with.

It's a common name, I tell myself. *It doesn't mean anything.*

But old habits die hard, and I file the information away.

Elena starts building the arrangement with sure, steady hands. She hums along with the music. "Silver Bells" is playing, and I find myself relaxing despite every instinct that tells me I shouldn't be here and a distraction I can't afford. Men like me don't get to stand in flower shops and watch beautiful women create art.

"You know what I love about flowers?" she suddenly questions, breaking the comfortable silence. "They're honest. A rose is always a rose. It doesn't pretend to be something it's not. It just is... beautiful, temporary, and real."

She looks up at me then, and there's something in her gaze that makes me think she's not just talking about flowers.

"People should be more like that," she continues. "Honest. Real. The world would be a better place, don't you think?"

I think about my world, where honesty gets you killed and being 'real' is a luxury no one can afford. Where I wear expensive suits like armor and keep my face carefully blank because showing emotion is a weakness.

"Perhaps," I say carefully.

She studies me for a long moment, her head tilted to one side. I have the uncomfortable sensation she's seeing right through me, past the expensive clothes and the cold mask, down to something I keep locked away.

"You're dangerous," she says finally, and my entire body goes tense. "Aren't you?"

Every muscle in my body coils, ready to move. My hand twitches toward the gun holstered at my side, hidden beneath my coat.

Does she know?

Has someone talked?

Is this a setup?

But then she laughs, a warm, musical sound that eases some of the tension in my shoulders.

"Not like that. I mean, you're dangerous to someone's heart. I bet you leave a trail of broken hearts everywhere you go." She shakes her head, returning to her arrangement. "Those intense, mysterious types always do."

Relief and something else, something warm and unexpected, floods through me.

She thinks I'm a heartbreaker.

If only she knew how laughable that is. I haven't had a relationship in years, haven't wanted one. My world doesn't allow for softness or connection. The women who pass through my life know the score—one night, maybe two if they're lucky, and then nothing.

No strings.

No complications.

No fucking flowers.

"I think you have the wrong idea about me," I say.

"Do I?" She positions a piece of pine with the precision of a surgeon. "You walked in here looking like you wanted to murder someone, wearing a suit that probably costs more than my rent, and you're buying flowers for your mother. Classic reformed bad-boy behavior."

"I'm *not* reformed."

The words come out harsher than I intended, and she looks up, startled. But then her expression softens into something that appears almost like understanding.

"No," she says quietly. "I don't suppose you are."

The moment stretches between us, loaded with something I can't quite name. Outside, the December sky is darkening, and the fairy lights strung throughout the shop glow warmer in response. Elena's face is shadowed and golden by turns, and I wonder what it would be like to trace the curve of her cheekbone with my thumb, to see if her skin is as soft as it looks.

I shouldn't be thinking these things.

I definitely shouldn't be feeling this pull toward her, this magnetic attraction that makes me want to stay in this flower shop forever, breathing in pine and cinnamon.

My phone vibrates in my pocket. Once. Twice. Three times.

Marco's emergency signal.

Fuck.

I pull it out, glancing at the screen. The message is brief.

Marco: *Greco spotted. Two blocks east. Three men.*

Sergio Greco. Underboss of the Russo family, the bastard who ordered the hit on my warehouse, and who's been systematically trying to provoke me into an all-out war.

And he's two blocks away from this flower shop.

From Elena.

I look up and find her watching me, a slight frown creasing her forehead.

"Is everything okay?"

"I have to go." I pull out my wallet, extracting several bills without counting them. It's too much, probably way too much, but I don't care. "Keep the change. Have the arrangement delivered to..." I pull out one of my business cards, the legitimate ones that list me as CEO of De Luca Imports. "This address."

She takes the card, her fingers brushing mine. The contact is brief, electric.

"Alessandro—"

"I'm sorry." And I am, more than she could possibly know. "I have to go. *Now*." I'm moving toward the door before she can respond, my hand already reaching for the weapon I pray I won't have to use.

Not here.

Not near *her*.

"Wait!"

I pause at the door, looking back despite knowing I shouldn't.

Elena is standing behind her worktable, holding my business card in one hand and a white amaryllis bloom in the other. In the warm glow of the fairy lights, with Christmas music playing softly and flowers surrounding her like a living painting, she looks like something out of a dream.

Something I have no right to want.

"Will you come back?" she asks.

I should say *no*. Should cut this off before it

13

begins, and I drag this beautiful woman into my dark world and ruin something pure and good.

"Yes," I say instead.

Her smile could light up the entire city.

"Good. I'll be here."

I push through the door into the December cold, the bell chiming behind me like a warning.

Marco is waiting at the corner, his expression grim. "Boss, we need to move. Greco's headed this way."

I cast one last look back at the shop. Through the frosted glass, I see Elena's silhouette as she returns to her work, completely unaware of the violence that stalks these streets. Unaware she just smiled at a monster, and said monster would burn the entire city down to keep her safe.

"Let's go," I tell Marco, falling into step beside him. "But we're not engaging. Not here."

"Boss—"

"Not here," I repeat, my tone leaving no room for argument.

Because two blocks isn't far enough. Not when she's standing in a shop full of windows, surrounded by delicate flowers and soft light. Not when the thought of a stray bullet finding her makes my blood run cold in a way that has nothing to do with the December weather.

We round the corner, and I catch sight of Greco and his men. They haven't seen us yet. We could take them, Marco and I, with the two men I have stationed in the car nearby.

We could end this here and now.

But I don't.

Instead, I watch them pass, memorizing faces, noting weapons, cataloging threats, planning for later when there's no flower shop full of warmth, light, and honey-eyed women nearby.

When we're clear, Marco looks at me like I've grown a second head.

"You want to tell me what the hell that was about?"

"Later," I say, pulling out my phone to text the rest of my team. "We'll deal with Greco on our terms, not his. Set up surveillance. I want to know everywhere he goes, everyone he talks to."

"Sure, boss. But that's not what I'm asking about." Marco has known me too long, seen too much. "You never back down from a fight, especially not with Greco. What's changed?"

I think about Elena—the way she looked at me like I was just a man instead of a monster, her talking about flowers being honest, people being real, and her asking if I'll come back.

"Nothing changed," I lie. "Just being strategic."

Marco doesn't believe me. I see it in his face, but he's smart enough not to push. We climb into the waiting car, and my driver pulls smoothly into traffic, already heading for my office downtown.

As we pull away from the curb, I catch a glimpse of Petals & Pines, its windows glowing warm against the dark street. And for a moment, I let myself imagine a different life. One where I could walk into that shop every day. Where I could make Elena laugh. Where I could be the kind of man who deserves someone like her.

But I'm not that man.

I'm Alessandro De Luca.

I've killed people.

I'll kill more.

My hands are stained with blood that no amount of flower-scented soap can wash clean.

And yet.

I pull out my phone and send a message to my assistant.

> **Me**: *Send white roses to Petals & Pines. Every week until I say otherwise.*

Then another message, this one to Marco.

> **Me**: *Find out everything about Elena Harper. But be discreet. I don't want her spooked.*

He reads it, raises an eyebrow at me, but simply nods.

The car merges into traffic, carrying me back

toward my world of shadows and violence. But my mind stays in the flower shop, wrapped in pine, cinnamon, and the memory of her beautiful eyes.

I'll go back.

I promised her.

What I didn't tell her is that I don't think I could stay away if I tried.

And that terrifies me more than any rival family ever could.

Chapter 2

Alessandro

Only thirty-six hours go by before I'm right back outside Petals & Pines.

Thirty-six hours of trying to convince myself that walking into her flower shop was a mistake.

Elena Harper is a distraction I can't afford. The way her honey-colored eyes lit up when she smiled at me means absolutely nothing in the grand scheme of my carefully ordered, violently maintained world.

Thirty-six hours of failing spectacularly at all of the above.

"Boss," Marco says from beside me, his tone carefully neutral in the way that means he thinks I've lost my mind. "You want to tell me why we're parked outside a flower shop on a Thursday afternoon?"

"No," I say, not taking my eyes off the storefront.

Through the frosted glass, there's movement, probably Elena, arranging flowers or helping a customer. The Christmas lights are on even though it's barely past noon, giving the whole shop a warm, inviting glow that stands in stark contrast to the gray December drizzle falling around us.

"Right. Okay. So we're just sitting here?"

"Surveillance," I tell him.

"Surveillance." Marco doesn't even try to hide his skepticism. "Of a flower shop."

"The area," I correct. "After Greco was spotted here two days ago, we need to ensure there are no additional threats in the vicinity."

It's not entirely bullshit. Greco being this close to my usual routes is concerning. The fact that he was two blocks from a place I'd just been is either a terrible coincidence or a calculated move on his part.

The fact that said place happens to be the flower shop owned by a woman I can't stop thinking about is just unfortunate timing.

"Uh-huh." Marco pulls out his phone, tapping away at something. "And the surveillance we've had on this street for the past two days wasn't enough?"

Dammit. I'd forgotten he'd see those orders.

"I'm being thorough."

"You're being something," he mutters, but wisely doesn't push further.

The truth is, I've read every report that's come in about this street. Every person who's walked past Petals & Pines. Every delivery truck that's stopped. Every customer who's gone in or out. I know Elena opens at nine, takes her lunch break around one—usually a sandwich from the deli three doors down—and closes at six. I know she had seventeen customers yesterday and twenty-three the day before. I know she lives alone in the apartment above the shop, and she hasn't had any visitors except for a blonde woman who appears to be a friend.

I know all of this, and it still isn't enough.

Which is how I find myself opening the car door and stepping out into the rain.

"Wait, we're going in?" Marco scrambles out after me. "Boss, what's the play here?"

Good question. I have no idea.

"Stay with the car," I tell him. "Keep your eyes open."

"For what?"

"Anything unusual."

Marco looks around at the perfectly ordinary downtown Seattle street, where people walk past with umbrellas, cars splash through puddles, and a guy stands across the street under an awning smoking a cigarette.

"Right. *Unusual.* Got it."

I ignore his tone and head for the shop, my heart doing something uncomfortably erratic in my chest. This is absurd. I've walked into hostile negotiations with Russian arms dealers and felt calmer than I do right now.

The bell chimes as I push through the door, and I'm hit with that same sensory overload as before— pine and cinnamon, warm light, explosions of color everywhere I look. And then I see *her*.

Elena is helping an older woman select roses, her hands gentle as she wraps the stems in brown paper. She's wearing jeans and a forest green sweater today, her hair is pulled back in a ponytail that makes her look impossibly young. When she laughs at something the customer says, a dimple appears in her left cheek.

My chest does something painful.

She hasn't seen me yet, so I take the opportunity to look around, pretending I'm browsing. The shop looks different in the daylight, somehow even more magical, if that's possible. There are new arrangements since I was here last, including a stunning display of white and red flowers in the window, which I'm certain wasn't there before.

"I think your grandson will love them," Elena is saying to the elderly woman. "Roses are classic for a reason."

"You're such a dear. Thank you, sweetie." The

woman pays and leaves, the bell chiming behind her.

And then Elena turns, and her eyes find mine.

For a second, she simply stares. Then her entire face lights up with a smile so bright it should probably come with a warning label.

"Alessandro! You came back!"

She sounds genuinely happy to see me. Not politely customer-service happy. Actually happy.

I'm so fucked.

"Hello, Elena."

"Did the arrangement arrive okay? Was your mother pleased?" She's already moving out from behind the counter, and I notice she's wearing the same worn boots as before. Something about that detail pleases me more than it should.

"It hasn't arrived yet," I say. "A family friend is flying back to Naples tomorrow. I arranged for the flowers to go with them." I smile. "I am sure she will love them, and she gets to see someone she hasn't seen in several years."

"Oh, good! I was a little nervous, you know, first time making something for a customer without knowing their exact preferences." She tucks a strand of hair behind her ear, and I notice she has small silver hoops in addition to the studs she was wearing before. "What brings you back? More flowers for your mom? Or maybe for someone else?"

There's something in her tone, not quite flirtatious, but curious. Interested.

"Actually," I say, and then stop because I realize I have no idea how to finish that sentence.

I came here to see you.

I haven't been able to stop thinking about you for two days.

I've been acting like a lovesick teenager, and it's making my second-in-command question my sanity.

None of these seems like a good option.

"Ribbon," I finally say.

She blinks. "Ribbon?"

"Yes. I need ribbon. For wrapping gifts."

Jesus Christ. Marco was right. I *have* lost my mind.

But Elena smiles, apparently finding nothing strange about a man in a three-thousand-dollar suit coming to a flower shop to buy ribbon.

"Oh, how thoughtful. Are you a wrapper, or do you usually pay people to do it?" She's already walking toward the back of the shop, and I follow like a moth to a flame. "I have to admit, I'm terrible at wrapping. I always use too much tape, and the corners never fold right. But ribbon... ribbon I can do."

She leads me to a section I didn't notice before, where spools of ribbon in every color imaginable hang from an old wooden rack. There must be fifty different options, from thin satin to thick velvet, in

23

solid colors and plaids, to designs with tiny Christmas trees.

"What's your style?" She pulls down a spool of deep burgundy velvet. "Classic? Modern? Rustic?"

I look at the ribbon, then at her, then back at the ribbon.

I have no fucking clue.

"Classic," I say, because it's worked before.

"Mmm." She studies me for a moment, her head tilted to one side. "Actually, I think you're more of a deep green person or maybe navy. Something rich and elegant but not obvious." She pulls down a spool of forest green velvet that matches her sweater. "Like this. It's sophisticated without being boring."

"I'll take it."

"Don't you want to know how much it is?"

"I'll take it," I repeat.

She laughs, it's a musical sound that does things to my chest. "Okay, big spender. How much do you need? I can cut you however many yards you want."

"Three yards," I say, pulling a number out of thin air.

"Three yards. Perfect." She pulls out scissors and starts measuring, humming along to the Christmas music playing in the background. Today it's "Let It Snow," and somehow she makes even that cheerful.

I should say something. Make conversation. This is what normal people do—*talk.*

"So," I start, then stop.

She looks up, waiting.

"You've owned this shop for two years?" It comes out more like an interrogation than a casual conversation. *Smooth, Alessandro. Real smooth.*

But she doesn't seem bothered and answers, "I opened in June, two and a half years ago. It was just a dream for a long time, but then I got a small business loan and found this space and..." She gestures around the shop with obvious pride. "Here we are."

"It's impressive." And I mean it. Building something from nothing and creating this warm and beautiful space takes courage and vision. "Did you always want to own a flower shop?"

"Since I was a kid." She starts cutting the ribbon, her movements precise. "My nonna, my grandmother, had the most amazing garden... roses, peonies, herbs, vegetables. She taught me that growing things was a way of putting beauty into the world. And I thought, why not make a living doing that?"

"Your grandmother sounds like a wise woman."

"She was."

Past tense.

Something flickers across Elena's face, grief, maybe, but softened by time. "She passed away five years ago. I think she would have loved this place."

"I'm sure she would have."

We fall into silence, but it's not uncomfortable. She finishes cutting the ribbon and carefully rolls it, securing it with a small piece of tape.

"There you go. Three yards of sophisticated, not boring forest-green ribbon." She hands it to me, and our fingers brush. The same electric jolt I felt before shoots through me.

She feels it too. I can tell by the way her eyes widen slightly and her cheeks flush.

"Thank you," I manage.

"Of course." She clears her throat, looking away. "Will that be all?"

No. I want to stay here forever, listening to you talk about your grandmother's garden and watching the way your eyes light up when you smile.

"Yes," I say instead.

We walk back to the register, I pull out my wallet, and she rings me up. The ribbon costs twelve dollars, which is probably the least expensive purchase I've made in years, and I hand her a hundred-dollar bill.

"Oh, I'll need to get change—"

"Keep it."

"Alessandro, I can't—"

"Consider it a tip. For *excellent* customer service."

She stares at me for a long moment, and I wonder if I've overstepped. But then she smiles, shaking her head.

"You know, you're a very strange man."

"So, I've been told."

"Strange in a good way," she clarifies. "Most people don't tip their florist. Or buy ribbon at a flower shop. Or show up looking like they're about to close a billion-dollar deal just to browse."

"I'm not most people."

"No," she says softly, studying me with those honey-colored eyes. "You're really not."

The moment stretches between us, loaded with something I can't quite name but can definitely feel. Outside, the rain has picked up, drumming against the windows. The Christmas lights cast shadows that dance across her face, and I find myself leaning slightly forward, drawn to her like gravity.

The bell above the door chimes.

We both jump, the spell broken.

A young couple enters, laughing and shaking rain from their coats, and Elena immediately shifts into professional mode.

"Welcome to Petals & Pines! Let me know if you need any help."

She glances back at me, and I see something in her expression, *regret, maybe, or perhaps disappointment* that the moment was interrupted.

I should leave. Let her help her customers. Go back to my car, where Marco is undoubtedly having a field day with whatever conclusions he's drawing.

But I don't want to.

"Elena," I say quietly, and she turns back to me. "Would you like to have coffee sometime?"

The words are out before I can stop them. Before I can think about all the reasons this is a terrible idea. Before I can remember, men like me don't date women like her.

She blinks, clearly surprised. "Coffee?"

"Or tea. Or lunch. Whatever you prefer." I'm making this worse. "I just thought we could talk. Get to know each other. If you're interested."

Say *no,* the rational part of my brain begs. Please, for your own safety, say *no.*

"I'd love to," she says, and her smile could power the entire city.

Fuck.

"Tomorrow?" I ask because apparently I'm committed to this disaster now. "I could pick you up after you close?"

"That would be perfect. Six fifteen?"

"Six fifteen," I confirm, memorizing the time like it's a tactical briefing.

"It's a date." She pauses. "It is a date. Not just coffee?"

The hopefulness in her voice does something to me.

Something dangerous.

"It's a date," I confirm.

Her smile gets impossibly wider. "Good. I'll see

you tomorrow then, Alessandro."

"Tomorrow," I repeat, then force myself to turn toward the door.

"Alessandro?" she calls after me.

I look back.

"You forgot your ribbon."

Right. The ribbon. The excuse I used to come here in the first place.

I walk back, take it from her outstretched hand. Our fingers brush again, and this time neither of us pulls away immediately.

"Tomorrow," she says again, softer this time.

"Tomorrow."

I manage to make it out of the shop without doing something stupid like kissing her in front of the young couple currently debating over poinsettias. The rain has picked up, coming down in sheets, but I barely notice it as I cross to where Marco is waiting by the car.

He takes one look at my face and starts laughing.

"Oh, this is beautiful. This is perfect. The great Alessandro De Luca brought down by a florist."

"Shut up," I mutter, sliding into the back seat.

"What'd you buy? More flowers?"

I hold up the ribbon.

Marco loses it completely, laughing so hard he has to lean against the car for support.

"Ribbon. You bought ribbon. Oh my God, wait until the guys hear about this."

"You tell anyone about this, and I'll have you running security at the fish market for a month."

That sobers him up. The fish market is our least profitable and least pleasant-smelling operation.

"Fine, fine. Your secret ribbon purchase is safe with me." He slides into the driver's seat, still grinning. "So did you at least get her number?"

"Better. I have a date with her tomorrow."

Marco's grin fades, replaced by concern. "Boss, I don't think that's a good idea."

"I didn't ask what you think."

"Yeah, well, I'm going to tell you anyway." He turns in his seat to face me. "You're at war with the Russo family. Greco is actively trying to provoke you into a confrontation. The last thing you need is a civilian girlfriend who could be used as leverage."

He's right, of course.

He's goddamn absolutely right.

"It's just coffee," I say.

"It's never *just coffee* with you. When was the last time you took a woman on a date? Actual date, not just screwing in the back of a club?"

I don't answer because I can't remember. Five years? Six?

Marco sighs. "Look, I get it. She's beautiful. She seems nice. But you know how this ends, right? Either you walk away and break her heart, or you don't walk away, and she becomes a target. There's no happy ending here."

"I'm aware of that."

"And you're doing it anyway?"

"Yes."

He studies me for a long moment, then shakes his head. "You're in deep already, aren't you?"

Am I? I've barely spoken to the woman. Two conversations, maybe fifteen minutes of total interaction. It's absurd to think I could be 'in deep' based on so little.

But then I remember the way she smiled at me, like I was someone worth smiling at. The way she talked about her grandmother's garden with such love. The way her eyes lit up when I asked her to coffee.

"Drive," I tell Marco.

He starts the car, muttering something in Italian that I choose to ignore. As we pull away from the curb, I look back at the shop one more time.

And freeze.

A man is standing across the street under an awning, partially obscured by shadows. He's watching the flower shop with an intensity that makes every instinct I have scream danger. He's wearing dark clothes, hands in his pockets, seemingly unbothered by the rain.

"Marco. Eleven o'clock. Black jacket."

Marco's eyes flick to the rearview mirror. "I see him."

"He was there when we arrived."

"You sure?"

I'm sure. I notice everything, especially potential threats. The man has been standing in roughly the same spot for over half an hour, barely moving, just watching.

"Circle back. I want to get a better look at him."

But by the time Marco navigates through traffic and comes back around, the man is gone.

"Probably nothing," Marco says, but he doesn't sound convinced.

"Add him to the surveillance reports. I want to know if he shows up again."

"You think he's one of Greco's?"

"I don't know." And that's what bothers me. In my business, unknown gets you killed. "But I want to find out."

Marco nods, already pulling out his phone to relay instructions to our surveillance team. I look back at Petals & Pines one more time as we drive away. Elena is visible through the window, helping the young couple, completely unaware that someone might be watching her, and I've probably painted a target on her back by showing interest.

Marco was right. There's no happy ending here. The smart thing would be to cancel tomorrow, to stay away from her, to let her live her life free from the violence that follows me like a shadow.

But I'm not going to do the smart thing.

I'm going to show up at six fifteen tomorrow,

take her for coffee, and pretend, for a little while, I'm the kind of man who gets to have normal things like dates, conversations, and maybe, eventually, something more.

And I'm going to make damn sure whoever was watching her shop today knows that Elena Harper is under my protection now.

Even if she doesn't know it yet.

3

Elena Harper

Only fifteen minutes to get ready, and it still turns into four outfit changes before Alessandro arrives.

This is ridiculous. I'm twenty-six years old, not some teenager getting ready for prom. But I can't help it, there's something about Alessandro De Luca that makes me feel like I'm standing on the edge of something big, terrifying, and wonderful all at once.

I finally settle on dark jeans, ankle boots, and a soft burgundy sweater, my best friend, Mira, swears makes my eyes look 'like liquid gold.' I leave my hair down in loose waves, add a touch of mascara and lip gloss, and try to ignore the butterflies doing acrobatics in my stomach.

At exactly six fifteen, and I mean exactly, like he

was watching the clock, there's a knock on the shop door.

I practically trip over my own feet racing down the stairs from my apartment.

He's standing outside in the rain, and oh my God, he looks even better than I remembered. Black coat, charcoal suit underneath, his dark hair slightly damp from the weather. But it's his eyes that catch me—dark, intense, and fixed on me through the glass like I'm the only thing in the world worth looking at.

I unlock the door and let him in, and immediately, the shop feels smaller. Not in a bad way, just in a way that makes me hyperaware of every breath, movement, and charged inch of space between us.

"Hi," I say, suddenly shy.

"Hello." His voice is rough velvet, and I feel it in places that are definitely not appropriate for a first date. "You look beautiful."

I feel my cheeks heat. "Thank you. You clean up pretty well yourself."

The corner of his mouth twitches, not quite a smile, but close. "I try."

We stand there for a moment, looking at each other, and I realize I have no idea what happens next. I've been on dates before, obviously, but none of them have felt like this. Like the air itself is electric.

"So," I say, tucking my hair behind my ear. "I was thinking about our coffee date, and I realized something."

"Oh?" He looks concerned, like he's bracing for me to cancel.

"Every coffee shop in the area is going to be packed on a Friday night. Loud music, no place to sit, people everywhere." I bite my lip, second-guessing myself even as the words come out. "Would you maybe want to come upstairs? To my apartment? I make really good coffee. And it's quiet. We could talk without having to shout at each other or read lips."

The moment the invitation leaves my mouth, I realize how it sounds. I just invited a man I barely know up to my apartment on our first date. My mother would have a heart attack. Mira would give me a lecture about stranger danger.

But Alessandro doesn't feel like a stranger. He feels like something *inevitable*.

"You're inviting me to your apartment," he says it slowly, carefully, like he's testing the words.

"I am. But if that's too forward, or if you'd rather go somewhere public, I completely understand."

"I'd love to."

The relief that floods through me is probably disproportionate to the situation.

"Great! Okay. It's just upstairs." I gesture toward the back of the shop where the stairs lead up to my apartment. "Fair warning, it's small and probably messy because I wasn't expecting company, but—"

"Elena," he says my name like it's something precious. "I'm sure it's perfect."

Oh, I am in so much trouble.

I lock the shop door behind us and lead him through the back room, past my worktable, supplies, and the industrial sink where I clean my tools, to the narrow staircase. I'm acutely aware of him behind me, his presence like heat at my back.

My apartment is exactly what you'd expect from someone who lives above a flower shop—small, cozy, and filled with plants. There are succulents on the windowsills, a fiddle leaf fig in the corner, and herbs growing in pots on the kitchen counter. The furniture is mostly secondhand, including a worn velvet couch in a dusty-rose color, a coffee table I refinished myself, and bookshelves made from reclaimed wood filled with paperbacks and vintage vases.

String lights are draped across the exposed brick wall, and a small Christmas tree stands in the corner, decorated with handmade ornaments and dried flowers. It's not fancy, but it's mine, and I love it.

Alessandro stops just inside the doorway, taking it all in. His expression is unreadable.

Oh God, he hates it.

It's too much.

Too cluttered.

"This is incredible," he says quietly.

I blink. "Really?"

"Really." He moves farther into the space, and I notice how out of place he looks, all sharp lines and expensive fabric in my soft, lived-in apartment. "It's very, *you*."

"Is that a good thing?"

He looks at me, and there's something in his eyes that makes my breath catch. "It's a very good thing."

Okay. Okay. I can do this. I can have a normal conversation with an incredibly attractive man in my apartment without spontaneously combusting.

"Coffee," I say, a little too brightly. "Let me make coffee."

I escape to the kitchen, which is really just an alcove with a stove, refrigerator, sink, and a small counter. My espresso machine, a splurge I justified because I'm Italian, and good coffee is non-negotiable, sits in pride of place on the counter, taking up most of the space.

"How do you take it?" I call over my shoulder.

"Black."

Of course he does. *Probably dark and bitter, like his soul.*

I immediately feel bad for thinking that. He hasn't been anything but polite and intense. *Very intense.*

"One black coffee coming up." I start the

machine, grateful for something to do with my hands. "I also have biscotti if you want, homemade. Well, Mira made them. She's the baker. I'm more of a kill-plants-and-bring-them-back-to-life person than a follow-recipes person."

I'm babbling. I'm definitely babbling.

"Biscotti sounds perfect."

I chance a glance at him, and find he's taken off his coat and is standing near my bookshelf, studying the spines. He looks more relaxed than I've seen him, though there's still something coiled about him as though he's ready to spring into action at any moment.

"You read a lot," he comments.

"Escapism is my drug of choice." I pull down my tin of biscotti and arrange some on a plate. "Romance, mostly. Some mystery. The occasional literary fiction when I'm feeling pretentious."

"No judgments on the romance novels."

"Why would there be? They're stories about people finding love and happiness. The world could use more of that." The espresso machine hisses, and I pour two cups. "Do you read?"

"When I have time. Mostly history. Biographies."

"Let me guess, military strategy? Sun Tzu? Machiavelli?"

He's quiet for a moment. "Yes, actually."

"Figures." I hand him his coffee and gesture to the couch. "You have that whole I've-read-The-

Prince-and-taken-notes vibe going on."

"Should I be offended?"

"Depends. Have you read The Prince?"

"Multiple times."

"Then no, you should be proud. It's very on-brand for you." I curl up on the opposite end of the couch, tucking my feet under me. "The mysterious, intense, possibly dangerous thing you've got going on."

Alessandro sits carefully, like he's afraid he might break something. He takes a sip of his coffee, and I watch his eyes close briefly in appreciation.

"This is excellent."

"I told you I made good coffee." I'm ridiculously pleased by his reaction. "So, Alessandro De Luca. Tell me about yourself. What do you do when you're not buying ribbon at flower shops?"

He goes still, and I realize I've hit on something. A nerve, maybe.

"I run an import business, De Luca Imports," he says it smoothly, but there's something rehearsed about it. "We deal primarily in goods from Europe."

"That sounds vague."

"It's not particularly interesting."

"Try me. I spend my days elbow-deep in dirt and flower stems. Trust me, everything sounds interesting compared to explaining the difference between ranunculus and peonies to confused customers."

He almost smiles. "What would you like to know?"

"I don't know. What do you import? Wine? Olive oil? Stolen artwork?"

I'm joking, obviously. But something flickers across his face. It's there and gone so quickly I almost miss it.

"Mostly wine and specialty foods," he says. "Some textiles. It's very boring, I promise."

He's lying or at least not telling me the whole truth.

The smart thing would be to press him on it. To demand answers about why a man who imports wine needs to wear a gun under his jacket. Yes, I noticed when he took his coat off, a slight bulk under his left arm, and that he looks at my windows as though he's calculating exit strategies.

But I don't want to be smart right now. I want to have coffee with a handsome man who makes my heart race and my skin feel too tight.

"Okay, boring-import-business guy," I say, taking a sip of my coffee. "What do you do for fun? When you're not working?"

He looks genuinely stumped by this question.

"Fun," he repeats, like it's a foreign concept.

"Yeah, you know. Hobbies? Interests? Things that make you happy?"

"I work."

"That's not a hobby, Alessandro. That's a lifestyle

41

choice, and not a particularly healthy one."

"I go to the gym."

"Also, not a hobby. That's exercise."

"I..." He pauses, and I can practically see him searching for an answer. "I don't know."

My heart does something painful in my chest. This man, this intense, mysterious, probably dangerous man, doesn't know what he does for fun.

"Okay, we're going to fix that," I declare. "Starting now. Quick, what's your favorite color?"

"I don't—"

"Don't think. Just answer."

"Red," he says, and looks as surprised as I am. "Dark red. Like your sweater."

Oh. Oh no. The butterflies are back, and they've brought friends.

"Favorite food?"

"My mother's carbonara."

"Favorite season?"

"Fall."

"Morning person or night person?"

"Night."

"Coffee or tea?"

"Coffee."

"Dogs or cats?"

"Dogs. Big ones."

I'm grinning now, watching him relax incrementally with each answer. "See? You can do fun. You just need practice."

"Is this what normal people do on dates?" He looks genuinely curious. "Rapid-fire questions?"

"This is what I do on dates. I find small talk boring. I want to know the real things. Like…" I grab a biscotti and point it at him. "If you could have dinner with anyone, living or dead, who would it be?"

"My father."

The answer comes quickly, and there's something raw in his voice that makes me want to reach across the couch and take his hand.

"Past tense," I say softly.

"He died when I was sixteen."

"I'm sorry."

"Don't be. He lived the life he chose." There's something complicated in his expression, like grief, anger, and something that might be pride. "Your turn. Who would you have dinner with?"

"My nonna. Without question." I smile at the memory. "She was this tiny Italian woman with an iron will and the greenest thumb I've ever seen. She could make anything grow. And she made the best tiramisu in the world. Don't tell my mother I said that."

"Your secret is safe with me."

We fall into an easier rhythm after that, trading questions and stories. I learn he's an only child who speaks Italian, English, and Spanish, has never been married, and has no children. He learns I'm terrible at math, that I once accidentally dyed all my white clothes pink in the laundry, and I'm afraid of spiders but will relocate them outside rather than kill them because *'they're just doing their spider thing.'*

He asks about my shop, and I light up talking about it, the joy of creating arrangements, helping people mark important moments with flowers, and the satisfaction of building something with my own hands.

"You love it," he observes.

"I do. It's hard work, and the margins are terrible, and I'm constantly worried about making rent, but..." I shrug. "It's mine. I created it. Every flower, every arrangement, every satisfied customer, that's all me. How many people get to say that about their work?"

"Not many."

"What about you? Do you love what you do?"

He's quiet for a long moment. "It's complicated."

"Most important things are."

"Yes." He's watching me with those intense dark eyes again, and I feel pinned in place. "You're very easy to talk to."

"Is that surprising?"

"Yes. I don't usually..." he trails off, seeming to struggle for words. "I don't do this. Dates. Conversation. Normal."

"Well, you're doing great." And I mean it. Yes, he's a bit awkward. Yes, there's something dangerous about him I can't quite put my finger on, but he's also genuine in a way most men I've dated aren't. He's not trying to impress me with money or connections. He's just here. Present. Listening like what I have to say matters.

"Thank you for inviting me up here," he says quietly. "For sharing this space with me. I know you don't know me very well, and it was probably not the smartest decision—"

"Hey." I lean closer, placing my coffee cup down with a soft click. "I know people, and everything about you says you're a good man, Alessandro De Luca. Complicated, secretive, ridiculously hot in those suits that probably cost more than my rent. And the way you keep eyeing my windows? I'm not sure if you're planning an escape or imagining how fast you could throw me out of one."

He goes very still. "You noticed that?"

"I notice a lot of things. I also noticed the gun under your jacket."

For a moment, I think he's going to leave. Or lie. Or both.

Instead, he says, "I should probably explain—"

The explosion cuts him off.

One second, we're sitting on my couch, having coffee and conversation, and the next, the entire building shakes. The windows rattle. My Christmas tree tips over. And the sound, God, the sound is deafening, like thunder, breaking glass, and destruction all rolled into one.

I scream.

I can't help it.

Alessandro is on his feet instantly, moving toward the window with a speed that shouldn't be possible. His whole demeanor has changed. He's no longer the awkward man struggling with small talk. In his place is someone cold, controlled, and terrifying.

"Stay away from the windows," he barks, his voice sharp with command.

I scramble off the couch, my heart hammering. "What was that? What's happening?"

He's on his phone, speaking in rapid Italian. Through the window, I see smoke rising from somewhere down the street. People are running, screaming, and car alarms are blaring.

"Alessandro—"

"Stay here." He's already moving toward the door, shrugging into his coat. "Lock the door behind me. Don't open it for anyone except me."

"Wait, what? You can't just leave."

He turns back, and the look on his face stops me cold. This is not the man who was just sitting on my couch, hesitantly answering questions about his favorite color. This is someone else entirely. Someone dangerous.

"Elena." He crosses back to me in two strides, taking my face in his hands. His touch is gentle despite the urgency in his voice. "I need you to listen to me very carefully. Lock the door. Stay away from the windows. Do not leave this apartment until I come back for you. Do you understand?"

"You're scaring me."

"Good. You should be scared. But you'll be safe if you do exactly as I say." His thumbs brush across my cheekbones, and for a second, I see something in his eyes, regret, maybe, or an apology? "I'm sorry. I'm so sorry. But I have to go."

"Alessandro—"

He kisses me.

It's brief, fierce, and completely unexpected. His lips are warm and firm against mine, and there's a desperation to it that makes my chest ache. And then he's pulling away, already moving toward the door. "Lock it behind me," he says again.

And then... he's gone.

Thundering down the stairs, leaving me standing in my suddenly-too-quiet apartment with the taste of him on my lips and the sound of chaos on the street below.

I lock the door with shaking hands.

Through the window, even though he told me to stay away from them, there's smoke billowing up from down the street. Sirens now sound, distant but getting closer. People are still running, still screaming.

And Alessandro is heading straight toward it.

I sink onto the couch, my mind racing.

What the hell just happened?

What was that explosion?

And why did Alessandro react like he was expecting it?

My phone buzzes.

Mira: *Are you okay? I heard an explosion near your shop.*

I stare at the message, not sure how to respond. *Am I okay?* I don't know. I'm unharmed, but I'm definitely *not* okay.

Another text comes through.

Unknown Number: *This is Alessandro. I'm sorry. I'll explain everything when I get back. Stay inside. Please.*

Clutching my phone, I'm torn between terror, confusion, and something else, something warm and fluttering that has no business existing in a moment like this. Because despite everything, the explosion, the gun, the way he transformed into someone cold and dangerous in the span of a heartbeat, I'm not afraid of Alessandro.

I'm afraid for him.

And that might be the scariest thing of all.
I text back.

Me: *Be careful.*

The response comes immediately.

Alessandro: *Always.*

I move away from the window and curl up on the couch, pulling a blanket around myself. My coffee has gone cold. The biscotti sits untouched on the plate. My Christmas tree is on its side, ornaments scattered across the floor.

Outside, the sirens are getting louder.

And all I can do is wait for a man I barely know to come back from whatever danger he's running toward.

A man who kissed me like it might be the last time.

A man who told me to lock the door and stay safe.

A man who, despite all my instincts screaming I should be terrified of, I think I might already be falling for.

I pull the blanket tighter and close my eyes.

Please be okay, Alessandro. Please come back.

Because I have questions.

So many questions.

And I have a feeling the answers are going to change everything.

Alessandro

There was no going back to Elena's apartment last night.

By the time the aftermath of the explosion was handled, Greco's pathetic little message, a blown-up car, two of my men injured but alive, it was three in the morning. She didn't need me showing up at her door covered in soot, blood, and barely contained rage.

So I sent her a text.

> **Me**: *Something came up. I'm sorry. Are you okay?*

Her response came immediately, like she'd been waiting.

Elena: *I'm fine. Are YOU okay?*
Me: *Yes. I'll explain everything. I promise.*

I didn't sleep. Instead, I spent the night in my office, tracking down every piece of information about the attack. Greco is getting bolder, more reckless. The explosion was two blocks from Elena's shop. Two blocks from where she lives.

Too close.

Marco tried to talk sense into me around four a.m. "Boss, you need to walk away from this girl. Greco knows about her now. He has to. Why else would he hit that location?"

"We have three properties within a five-block radius of the explosion," I pointed out. "It doesn't mean anything."

"It means he's sending you a message. And the message is *nothing you care about is safe.*"

The problem is, Marco is right. I should walk away. Ghost her. Let her think I'm just another asshole who kissed her and disappeared.

But I can't.

Which is how I find myself standing outside Petals & Pines at exactly six p.m. the next evening, holding a bouquet of roses that's probably three times larger than it needs to be.

I went overboard, and I know it.

But after last night, leaving her alone and terrified, after putting her in danger just by being near her, I needed to do something grand. Something that shows her how sorry I am. How much I want to make this right.

So, I bought out half a flower wholesaler. Three dozen long-stem red roses, arranged with some feathery green stuff and tied with a silk ribbon. The florist, not Elena, obviously, since that would defeat the purpose, assured me it was *appropriately romantic without being overwhelming.'*

Looking at it now, it's definitely overwhelming.

My car is parked at the curb, the Mercedes, not the SUV I usually use for business. My driver, Paulo, is behind the wheel, waiting patiently. I'm wearing my best suit, Armani, charcoal gray with a black shirt underneath. No tie, because I read somewhere that ties are too formal for dinner dates.

I have reservations at Canlis, the best restaurant in Seattle, with waterfront views, seven courses, and wine pairings. I pulled every string I have to get a table on twenty-four hours' notice.

Marco, who watched me prepare for this evening with increasing horror, told me I looked like I was either closing a hostile merger or attending a funeral.

He might have a point.

The shop door is locked, she closes at six, but there's movement inside. Elena is cleaning up for the day. My chest does that uncomfortable thing it's been doing since I met her, like my heart is trying to remember how to feel something other than cold calculation.

I knock.

She looks up, and even through the frosted glass, I see her smile. That dimple in her left cheek. Those honey-colored eyes that see too much.

She unlocks the door and opens it, and I'm struck all over again by how beautiful she is. She's wearing jeans and a simple white sweater, her hair in a ponytail. No makeup that I can see. She looks *perfect*.

And then she sees the roses.

"Oh my God," she says.

"I wanted to apologize for last night." I thrust the bouquet toward her. "For leaving so abruptly. For not coming back. For—"

"Alessandro, this is..." She takes the roses and pauses, her eyes wide. "This is a lot of roses."

"Too much?"

"I mean, it's definitely a statement." She buries her face in the blooms, inhaling. When she looks back up, she's trying not to laugh. "What exactly are you apologizing for? Because this feels like I-crashed-your-car level of apology flowers, not I-had-to-leave-during-an-emergency flowers."

"I wanted to make it up to you."

"With three dozen roses."

"Is that too many?"

"There's no such thing as too many roses when

you own a flower shop." She steps aside, gesturing for me to come in. "Give me one second to put these in water. They're beautiful, by the way. Excessive, but beautiful."

I follow her inside, watching as she expertly trims the stems and arranges them in a large vase. Her movements are practiced and efficient. She makes it look easy.

"So," she says, not looking at me. "Last night was intense."

"I'm sorry."

"Stop apologizing. I'm fine. A little shaken up but fine." She finishes with the roses and turns to face me. "I'm more worried about you. That explosion was close. And you ran toward it."

"It was my responsibility."

"Your responsibility?" She tilts her head, studying me. "Alessandro, what do you really do? And please don't tell me you import olive oil because olive oil importers don't carry guns or run toward explosions."

This is it. The moment when I should tell her the truth, explain exactly what kind of man I am, and give her the chance to run.

"It's complicated," I say instead.

"You keep saying that."

"Because it's true."

She sighs, then seems to make a decision. "Okay. You don't want to talk about it right now, I get it.

But eventually, Alessandro, you're going to have to trust me with the truth. Because I really like you, and I can't keep dating someone who's hiding something this big."

She likes me. The words do something warm and dangerous to my chest.

"I will," I promise. "I'll tell you everything, just not tonight. Tonight, I want to take you to dinner and try to have a normal date. If you'll still go with me after I abandoned you last night."

"Of course I'll go with you." She reaches out and touches my arm, and even through the layers of my suit, I feel it like a brand. "But can I just change quickly? I didn't realize we were doing a fancy dinner. I thought maybe pizza or something casual."

I look down at my suit, then at her jeans and sweater. "You look perfect."

"Alessandro, you're wearing Armani. I'm wearing Target. There's a slight disparity here."

"I don't care what you wear."

"But I do." She's already moving toward the stairs. "Give me ten minutes. There's coffee in the pot if you want some."

She disappears upstairs before I can protest, leaving me standing in her flower shop surrounded by the smell of roses and pine.

I pull out my phone and text Marco.

Me: *She thinks I overdid it.*

His response is immediate.

Marco: *You THINK? Boss, you look like you're taking her to meet the Pope, not to dinner. Too late to change now. Good luck. You're going to need it.*

I'm starting to think he's right.

Elena comes back down exactly ten minutes later, and I forget how to breathe.

She's changed into a black dress that hits just above her knees, simple and elegant. Her hair is down now, falling in waves around her shoulders. She's added heels that make her legs look endless and a touch of lipstick that makes me want to kiss her until it's smeared beyond recognition.

"Better?" she asks, doing a little spin.

"You're stunning," I manage to say.

She blushes. "You're not so bad yourself. Very GQ. Very I-own-a-yacht-and-make-business-deals-over-scotch."

"I don't own a yacht."

"But you do make business deals over scotch?"

"Sometimes."

She grabs a small purse and a coat. "Where are we going?"

"Canlis."

Her eyes widen. "Canlis? Alessandro, that place is impossible to get into. How did you... never mind. Olive oil importing must pay really well."

If she only knew.

Paulo is waiting by the car when we step outside. He opens the back door with perfect professional courtesy, not meeting my eyes. *Smart man.*

Elena stops dead when she sees him.

"You have a driver."

"Yes."

"You have a driver and a Mercedes and reservations at Canlis." She looks at me, something between amusement and exasperation on her face. "This is a bit much, don't you think?"

"I wanted to do this properly."

"Properly would have been picking me up in your own car and taking me somewhere we could talk without seven forks and a sommelier."

"There won't be seven forks. Maybe five."

"Alessandro." She steps closer, lowering her voice. "I appreciate the gesture, I really do. But I don't need all this. I only need you."

The words hit me square in the chest. She doesn't need the money, the power, or the carefully constructed image I've spent years building. She only needs me.

The problem is, she doesn't know what *'me'* actually entails.

"Get in the car," I say softly. "Please. Let me do

this. Let me try to make up for last night."

She studies me for a long moment, then sighs. "Fine. But next time, we're getting pizza. In jeans. Like normal people."

"Deal."

She slides into the car, and I follow, acutely aware of how close we are in the back seat. I can smell her perfume. It's something light and floral with a hint of vanilla. It's intoxicating.

Paulo pulls away from the curb, and I force myself to focus on conversation instead of how much I want to pull her into my lap.

"So," Elena says, turning to face me. "Tell me more about you. Not work stuff. Real stuff. What's your favorite movie?"

"I don't watch many movies."

"Everyone has a favorite movie."

"*The Godfather*."

She bursts out laughing. "Of course it is. Of course. Let me guess, you can relate to Michael Corleone?"

More than she knows.

"It's a well-made film," I say defensively.

"It's about the mafia, Alessandro. Murder, betrayal, and family loyalty taken to criminal extremes."

"It's about a man trying to protect what's his."

She's quiet for a moment, and when she speaks again, her voice is softer. "Is that what you're doing?

Protecting what's yours?"

"Always."

The word hangs between us, loaded with meaning I can't quite articulate. She doesn't press, just nods as though she understands something I haven't said.

We make small talk for the rest of the drive. She tells me about a difficult customer who wanted roses but only from a specific farm in Ecuador. I tell her about a shipment of wine that got held up in customs for three weeks. It's easy, comfortable, and I find myself relaxing despite the oversized roses, the suit, and the driver.

Maybe this will be okay.

Maybe I can have one normal evening with her before everything inevitably falls apart.

Canlis is perched on a hill overlooking Lake Union, all glass and mid-century modern elegance. Paulo drops us off at the entrance, and a valet immediately appears to open Elena's door.

"I'll be nearby," Paulo says quietly to me. "If you need anything."

What he means is, I'll be watching for threats. I'll be armed. I'll be ready.

"Thank you," I tell him.

Inside, the maître d' greets us with perfect professional warmth. "Mr. De Luca, welcome. Your table is ready."

He leads us through the dining room, all warm

wood with soft lighting and floor-to-ceiling windows with views of the city lights reflected on the water. It's beautiful. Romantic. Exactly what I wanted.

Our table is in the corner, slightly secluded and private.

Elena's eyes are wide as she takes it all in. "This is incredible."

"I'm glad you like it." I hold her chair out for her, and she sits with a small smile.

"Such a gentleman."

"I try."

The sommelier appears with a wine list that's practically a novel. I order a bottle of Barolo without looking at the prices, and Elena raises an eyebrow but doesn't comment.

"So," she says once we're alone again. "Do you do this often? The fancy restaurant, the driver, the full romantic treatment?"

"No. Never."

"Never?"

"You're the first woman I've taken to dinner in five years."

She blinks. "I'm sorry, what?"

"You heard me."

"But you're... you." She gestures at me like I'm a puzzle she can't figure out. "You're gorgeous and wealthy and mysterious. Women must throw themselves at you constantly."

"That's different."

"How?"

"Because those women don't matter." The words come out harsher than I intended. "They're not... this isn't..."

"Alessandro." Her hand reaches across the table, finding mine. Her touch is warm, soft. "Breathe. You're doing fine."

But I'm not. Because sitting here with her in this beautiful restaurant with the city lights sparkling below us, I'm acutely aware of how much I want this. How much I want her. And how impossible it all is.

The waiter arrives with our wine and goes through the tasting ritual. I barely pay attention, too focused on the way Elena's thumb is tracing patterns on the back of my hand.

We order, she gets the halibut, I get the steak, and we fall into easy conversation. Elena tells me about her friend, Mira, who runs a bakery two streets over. I tell her about Marco, my second-in-command, though I frame him as my business partner.

"He sounds protective," she observes.

"He's known me for a long time."

"And he doesn't approve of me?"

I hesitate. "He doesn't think I should be dating anyone right now. Business is... complicated."

"There's that word again."

"I'll explain. Soon. I promise."

Our food arrives perfectly cooked and beautifully plated. Elena takes a bite of her halibut and actually moans, and the sound goes straight through me.

"Oh my God," she says. "This is amazing. Try it."

She holds out her fork, offering me a bite. It's intimate in a way that makes my heart race, sharing food, being close, this small domestic gesture.

I lean forward and take the bite, and she's right. It's incredible.

"Good?" she asks, her eyes sparkling.

"Very."

"Your turn." She nods at my steak. "Share."

I cut a piece and hold it out. She leans forward, her lips closing around the fork, and Jesus Christ, I need to think about something else before I do something inappropriate in the middle of Canlis.

"That's perfect," she moans. "Why doesn't food taste like this when I cook?"

"Maybe you're cooking the wrong things."

"Or maybe I'm just a terrible cook. Nonna tried to teach me, but I was always more interested in the garden than the kitchen." She takes a sip of wine. "What about you? Do you cook?"

"Sometimes. Basic things."

"Let me guess... pasta? Very traditional Italian dishes?"

"My carbonara is almost as good as my mother's."

"Almost?"

"You never tell an Italian mother your cooking is better than hers. It's a cardinal sin."

She laughs, and the sound fills me with warmth.

This is good.

This is working.

Maybe Marco was wrong.

Maybe I can have these dinners, conversations, and moments of normalcy in between the violence and the blood.

And then I see him.

Greco's man, standing near the bar. Dark suit, hand in his pocket. His eyes lock on mine, and I see the moment he recognizes me.

Fuck.

"Elena," I say carefully, not taking my eyes off the threat. "I need you to stay calm."

"What?" She starts to turn around.

"Don't look." My voice is sharp enough that she freezes. "Keep looking at me. Smile like we're having a wonderful time."

"Alessandro, you're scaring me."

"I know. I'm sorry. But I need you to trust me." I pull out my phone and text Paulo with practiced ease.

Me: *Greco's man inside. Need exit.*

Elena is staring at me, her face pale. "What's happening?"

"Nothing. Everything is fine. We're just going to leave a little early."

"You said we were having a wonderful time."

"We are. But something came up."

"Something always comes up with you," she says, and there's hurt in her voice now. "Every time we're together, something happens. The explosion, now this—"

A crash from the bar area cuts her off. I'm on my feet instantly, positioning myself between Elena and the threat. Greco's man is arguing with someone, one of my guys, I realize. Paulo must have sent him in.

"We need to go. *Now.*"

I grab Elena's hand and pull her toward the back of the restaurant. The maître d' moves to intercept, but one look at my face and he steps aside.

"Sir, is everything—"

"Emergency," I say shortly. "We'll settle the bill later."

I rush Elena through the kitchen as chefs and sous chefs jump out of our way, and out the back door into an alley. Paulo is already there with the car, engine running.

"In," I order.

Elena doesn't argue, sliding into the back seat. I follow, and Paulo peels out before my door is even fully closed.

"What the hell was that?" Elena demands. "Alessandro, what is going on?"

"There was a situation. I got us out of it."

"A situation? You mean the guy at the bar?"

"You said you weren't going to look."

"Yeah, well, I looked anyway." She's angry now, I can see it in the set of her jaw. "Who was he? Why did we have to run?"

Through the rear window, I notice another car pulling out of the alley behind us.

Greco's men, following.

"Paulo, lose them," I say quietly.

"On it, boss."

Elena's eyes widen. "Lose them? Lose who? Alessandro—"

Paulo takes a hard right, then a left, weaving through downtown streets with the practiced ease of someone who's done this before. The car behind us struggles to keep up.

"Hold on," Paulo warns.

He cuts across two lanes of traffic, earning angry honks, and ducks into a parking garage. He takes the turns fast, tires squealing, going up two levels before pulling into a spot and killing the engine.

We sit in silence for a moment, listening. Waiting.

No other car follows.

"We're clear," Paulo says.

"Good. Take us back to Elena's place. Different route."

"Wait." Elena's voice is small, scared. "We're going back to my apartment? What if they followed us there? What if—"

"They didn't follow us. Paulo lost them."

"Paulo lost them because he's done this before." She's looking at me now, really looking at me, and I see the pieces clicking into place. "Because this is normal for you. Having drivers who can lose people in car chases. Running out of restaurants. Carrying guns."

"Elena—"

"Tell me the truth." Her voice is shaking. "Right now. What do you really do, Alessandro?"

I could lie.

Should lie.

Tell her it's business rivalry, corporate espionage, anything but the truth.

But I'm tired of lying to her.

"I'll tell you everything," I say. "When we get you home safe. When you're behind a locked door, and I know you're protected. Then I'll tell you everything."

She stares at me for a long moment, then nods slowly. "Okay. But you promise? No more dodging, no more *'it's complicated.'* "

"I promise."

She leans back against the seat, and I see her

blinking back tears. "This was supposed to be a nice dinner."

"I know. I'm sorry."

"You apologize a lot."

"I have a lot to apologize for."

We drive back to her place in silence. Paulo takes a circuitous route, doubling back several times to make sure we're not followed. When we finally pull up outside Petals & Pines, it's fully dark, the shop windows glowing with Christmas lights.

"I'll walk you up," I say.

"You don't have to—"

"I'm walking you up."

She doesn't argue. Instead, Elena gets out of the car, opens her shop, and waits inside.

"Pull the door, it locks automatically."

I nod, and we climb the stairs to her apartment. The silence between us is heavy with unspoken words. She unlocks her door and steps inside, and I follow, checking the windows, the locks, making sure everything is secure.

"Alessandro." She's standing in the middle of her living room, still in that beautiful black dress, her arms wrapped around herself. "I need you to tell me the truth. All of it. Because I'm starting to really care about you, and I can't do that if I don't know who you really are."

I look at her, this beautiful, kind, honest woman who makes flower arrangements and believes in happy endings, and I know that what I'm about to tell her will change everything.

"I'm not just an importer," I say. "I'm the head of the De Luca family. We control most of the organized crime in Seattle... drugs, gambling, protection. All of it runs through me."

She doesn't say anything, only stares at me with those honey-colored eyes.

"The man at the restaurant works for a rival family. They're trying to move in on my territory, and they're using violence to do it. The explosion last night was them. The car chase tonight was them. And being near me puts you in danger."

"You're in the mafia?" she asks slowly.

"Yes."

"You're a criminal?"

"Yes."

"And those men, they want to hurt you?"

"They want to kill me. And they'll use anyone close to me to do it."

She sinks onto the couch, processing my words. I should leave. Give her space. Let her decide if she wants anything to do with me now that she knows the truth.

But I can't move. I need to know her reaction, even if it destroys me.

"Tonight," she finally says. "The fancy dinner, the driver, all of it was your way of apologizing for putting me in danger?"

"Yes."

"And the roses?"

"Those too."

She's quiet for another moment, then looks up at me. "You're an idiot."

Not what I expected.

"Elena—"

"You're a complete and total idiot, Alessandro De Luca." She stands up, crossing to where I'm standing. "I don't care about fancy restaurants or expensive wine or oversized bouquets. I care about this." She presses her hand to my chest, right over my heart. "I care about the man who loves his mother enough to buy her special flowers, asks about my grandmother's garden, and gets awkward when I ask about his hobbies. That's the man I'm falling for."

Falling for.

"You shouldn't," I say roughly. "You should run as far away from me as possible."

"Probably," she agrees. "But I'm not going to."

And then she kisses me.

Chapter 5

Elena

The kiss lasts exactly four seconds before Alessandro pulls away like he's been burned.

"We can't do this," he says, his voice rough. He's still close enough that his breath ghosts across my lips. "Elena, you don't understand what you're getting into."

"You're in the mafia. You deal with dangerous people. Someone might try to hurt me to get to you." My heart is hammering, but my voice stays steady. "Did I miss anything?"

"It's not that simple—"

"It's exactly that simple. You're dangerous. I'm probably insane for not running screaming. But here's the thing, Alessandro, I'm a grown woman who can make her own decisions. And I'm deciding I want to keep seeing you."

He stares at me as if I've grown a second head. "You could get hurt."

"I could get hit by a bus tomorrow. Life doesn't come with guarantees."

"This is different."

"Is it?" I step closer, emboldened by the way his eyes darken when I do. "Because from where I'm standing, you're offering me honesty. *Real honesty.* How many relationships start with complete transparency about the ugly parts?"

"Most relationships don't involve organized crime."

"True. But most relationships don't involve three-dozen-rose apologies either, so we're already off to a unique start."

The corner of his mouth twitches. Almost a smile. "You're insane."

"Probably. But I'm also stubborn as hell, ask anyone who knows me, and when I want something, I don't give up easily." I reach up and touch his face, feeling the scratch of stubble under my palm. "I want this. I want you. Even knowing what I know."

"Elena—"

"Stop trying to protect me from yourself. Let me make my own choices." My thumb brushes across his cheekbone. "Unless you don't want this? Unless I'm reading this all wrong and you're trying to let me down easy?"

His hands come up to grip my waist, pulling me closer. "You're not reading it wrong."

"Then stop arguing with me."

"I don't think you understand how difficult that is." But there's warmth in his eyes now, something almost like wonder. "You should be afraid of me."

"Maybe I should be, but I'm not." And it's true. Standing here in my apartment with a confessed crime boss, I feel safer than I have with any other man. "Here's what's going to happen. We're going to keep dating, but on my terms this time."

"Your terms?"

"My terms. Which means no more fancy restaurants where people try to kill you. No more drivers. No more oversized romantic gestures." I poke him in the chest. "Next time, we do something normal. Something fun. Something where you can't brood in an Armani suit."

"I don't brood."

"You absolutely brood. It's one of your most defining characteristics."

He almost smiles again. "What did you have in mind?"

"The Christmas market in Pike Place. Tomorrow night. We'll get hot chocolate, look at overpriced crafts, and you can win me a stuffed animal at one of those rigged carnival games."

"That sounds..."

"Normal? Boring? Not nearly dramatic enough

for a mafia boss?"

"Perfect," he says quietly. "It sounds perfect."

The word hangs between us, warm and promising. He's still holding my waist, his thumbs making small circles that send sparks up my spine.

"You should go," I whisper, even though leaving is the last thing I want him to do.

"I should."

Neither of us moves.

"Alessandro."

"Mmm?"

"If you don't leave now, I'm going to kiss you again. And then I'm going to invite you to stay. And then…" I trail off, suddenly shy.

His eyes go almost black. "And then?"

"And then I think we both know where this would go. But I don't want that yet. Not until I'm sure you're not going to disappear on me the moment things get complicated."

"Things are already complicated."

"More complicated, then."

He leans his forehead against mine, breathing hard. "You're killing me."

"Good. Consider it payback for the emotional whiplash of the past three days."

This time, he does smile, a real smile that transforms his whole face. "Tomorrow night. The Christmas market."

"Six o'clock. And Alessandro? Wear jeans."

"I don't think I own jeans."

"Then buy some. No suits allowed."

He kisses my forehead. It's soft, sweet, devastating, and then he's gone, leaving me standing alone in my apartment with my heart racing, my lips tingling, and the distinct feeling my life has gone completely off the rails.

Mira is going to lose her mind when I tell her.

The next evening, I changed my outfit three times before settling on dark jeans, boots, and a cream-colored sweater under my favorite red coat. My hair is down and wavy, and I've added actual makeup this time, including mascara, a touch of blush, lipstick in a shade called 'Kiss Me if You Dare.'

Maybe I'm being too obvious.

At precisely six o'clock, because of course he's exactly on time, there's a knock at the shop door.

When I open it, my jaw nearly drops.

Alessandro De Luca is wearing jeans.

Dark wash, perfectly fitted, paired with a black Henley and a charcoal wool coat. His hair is slightly less styled than usual, and he looks, *God help me*, he looks edible.

"You own jeans," I manage.

"I bought them this afternoon." He does a self-conscious half turn. "Are they acceptable?"

"They're more than acceptable." *Understatement of the century*. "You look good. Really good."

"So do you." His eyes travel over me slowly, appreciatively, and heat pools low in my belly. "Beautiful."

"Flatterer."

"Honest." He offers his arm. "Shall we?"

The Christmas market at Pike Place is packed with people, couples holding hands, families with kids sticky from candy canes, tourists taking photographs of the lights. The air smells of roasted chestnuts and cinnamon, and every booth plays different Christmas music, creating a cheerful cacophony.

Alessandro looks like he's been dropped into an alien landscape.

"There are so many people," he mutters, his hand finding the small of my back as we navigate through the crowd.

"It's a popular event. Come on, let's get hot chocolate."

We wait in line at a booth decorated with twinkling lights and artificial snow. Alessandro keeps scanning the crowd, his body tense, and I realize he's not overwhelmed by the people but assessing threats.

"Hey." I touch his arm. "We're safe here. It's a public place with families and security and about a thousand witnesses."

"That's what worries me."

"Alessandro. Look at me..." When he does, I see the concern in his dark eyes. "I need you to try to relax. Just for tonight. Can you do that?"

He takes a deep breath, then nods. "I can try."

We order hot chocolate, extra whipped cream for me, dark chocolate for him, and wander through the market. The stalls are filled with handmade ornaments, knitted scarves, artisan soaps, and wooden toys. Everything is decorated with pine boughs, red ribbons, and fairy lights, creating a magical atmosphere.

"This is nice," Alessandro admits after we've been walking for a while. He's relaxing incrementally, his shoulders no longer rigid. "I haven't done something like this in years."

"When was the last time?"

"I was maybe ten. My father took me to a Christmas market in Naples." There's fondness in his voice, but also sadness. "He bought me roasted chestnuts and let me stay up past my bedtime looking at the lights."

"That's a good memory."

"One of the last good ones, before..." he trails off.

"Before he died?"

"Before everything changed." He stops at a booth selling wooden ornaments, picking up a hand-carved angel. "He wasn't always in the life. He tried to go legitimate when I was young, but the family pulled him back in."

"The family. You mean—"

"The mafia, yes. It's… it's hard to leave. Once you're in, you're in for life." He sets the angel down carefully. "I didn't have a choice. When he died, the business became mine. The responsibilities, the territory, the blood… all of it."

My heart aches for him. For the boy who lost his father and inherited a nightmare. "Alessandro—"

"You should know what you're getting into," he continues, still not looking at me. "I can't just walk away. This is my life, full of violence, danger, and difficult choices. I can try to keep you separate from it, but eventually, the two worlds *will* collide. They always do."

"Then we'll deal with it when it happens."

"Elena—"

"No." I step in front of him, forcing him to meet my eyes. "I heard you. I understand the risks. And I'm still here. Can we please enjoy tonight? Can we pretend, even for a few hours, we're normal people on a normal date at a Christmas market?"

He studies my face for a long moment, then something in him softens. "Okay."

"Okay?"

"Okay. Normal date. Normal people." He takes my hand, lacing our fingers together. "Where to next?"

We spend the next hour exploring. Alessandro wins me a stuffed penguin at the ring toss. It takes him six tries, and the competitive gleam in his eyes makes me laugh. We sample fudge from a chocolate booth, and I discover he has a secret sweet tooth. We look at hand-blown glass ornaments, and he buys me a delicate snowflake before I can protest.

"For your tree," he says.

"You're going to spoil me."

"That's the plan."

The way he says it, very casual but completely sincere, makes my stomach flutter.

We end up near the center of the market, where strings of fairy lights are draped overhead in a canopy of twinkling gold. An acoustic guitarist is playing "Silent Night," and a few couples are swaying together despite the lack of a dance floor.

"Dance with me," Alessandro says suddenly.

"Here? Now?"

"Why not? You wanted normal." He pulls me closer, one hand on my waist, the other still holding mine. "This is normal."

"You're full of surprises tonight."

"Good surprises?"

"The best kind."

We sway together, not quite in time with the music, surrounded by strangers, Christmas lights, and the soft fall of snowflakes drifting down from the dark sky.

"It's snowing," I whisper, tipping my head back to watch the flakes spiral down.

"So it is."

When I look back at him, he's not watching the snow. He's watching me, his expression soft in a way I've never seen before.

"What?" I ask.

"You're beautiful." He reaches up and brushes a snowflake from my eyelash. "You're standing here in the snow with a stuffed penguin tucked under your arm, covered in hot chocolate and smiling like this is the best night of your life, and you're the most beautiful thing I've ever seen."

My breath catches. "Alessandro…"

"I'm going to kiss you now." His voice is low, intimate. "If that's okay."

"More than okay," I breathe out.

He leans down slowly, giving me time to pull away if I want to, but I don't want to. I rise on my toes to meet him halfway, my free hand curling into his coat.

When his lips meet mine, the entire world narrows to this moment. This man. This kiss.

It's nothing like the desperate, hurried kiss in my apartment. This is slow, deep, and thorough, as though Alessandro's memorizing the taste of me. His hand slides into my hair, tilting my head to deepen the angle. I make a slight sound in the back of my throat, and he responds by pulling me impossibly closer.

Someone whistles nearby, and I vaguely register we're making a scene, but I don't care. Nothing exists except Alessandro's mouth on mine, his hand in my hair, and the solid warmth of his body against mine.

When we finally break apart, we're both breathing hard. Snowflakes have collected in his dark hair, and his lips are slightly swollen from kissing me.

"Wow," I whisper.

"Wow," he agrees.

The guitarist has moved on to "White Christmas," and the world has resumed spinning. But something has shifted between us. Something permanent, meaningful, and terrifying in the best way.

"Elena," he starts, his voice rough with emotion.

The crack of a gunshot shatters the moment.

Everything happens in a rush. Alessandro's body slams into mine, taking me down to the cold ground. His weight crushes me, protective and immovable. Around us, people are screaming, running, chaos erupting as though a bomb has gone off.

"Stay down," Alessandro growls in my ear. "Don't move."

My mind can't process what's happening. One second, we were kissing under fairy lights. Now we're on the ground, Alessandro covering me completely, people are running and screaming, and—

Another shot.

Closer this time.

Alessandro shifts, his hand going to his jacket. When it comes back, he's holding a gun.

He has a gun at the Christmas market.

He brought a gun on our date.

"Alessandro—"

"Not now." His voice is steel. His eyes scan the crowd, the rooftops, looking for something I can't see. "Paulo, where are you?"

He must have an earpiece. Of course, he has an earpiece. Of course, he brought security to the Christmas market because he's a mafia boss who can't even take his girlfriend on a normal date without someone trying to kill him.

Girlfriend. Am I his girlfriend? Is now really the time to be thinking about labels?

"Shooter on the north roof," Alessandro says, his voice calm despite the chaos. "Red building. Do you have a visual?"

A pause.

"Take the shot."

My stomach drops. He's ordering someone to shoot another person, to kill them, while lying on top of me at a Christmas market, where five seconds ago we were kissing in the snow.

"We need to move," Alessandro says to me, his voice gentler now. "Can you move?"

"I... yes. I think so."

"Good. When I say go, we're going to run to that booth." He nods toward a sturdy wooden structure selling Christmas trees. "Stay low, stay behind me, and don't stop moving. Understand?"

"Alessandro, what's happening—"

"Elena." His eyes lock on mine, and I see fear there—real, raw fear. "I need you to trust me. Can you do that?"

Can I? Can I trust this man who brought a gun to our date, who's currently calling in hits while pinning me to the snowy ground of Pike Place Market?

But when I look into his eyes, I see the truth.

He's terrified, not for himself, but for me.

"I trust you," I whisper.

"Good. On three. One... two... three... *go!*"

We move. Alessandro hauls me up and pushes me forward, his body between me and wherever that shooter is. We run, awkward, crouched, my boots slipping on the snow-slicked ground. The Christmas tree booth is maybe twenty feet away, but it feels like miles.

Another shot rings out. The wooden post next to my head explodes in splinters.

Alessandro makes a sound of either pain or anger, I can't tell, and then we're diving behind the booth, hitting the ground hard enough to knock the air from my lungs.

"You okay?" He's immediately checking me over, hands running over my arms and ribs, looking for injuries. "Did you get hit? Elena, talk to me."

"I'm fine. I'm fine." The words come out shaky. "Are you okay?"

"I'm fine."

But when I look down, there's blood on his coat. Not a lot, but enough.

"You're bleeding!"

"It's nothing. Only a graze."

"You got shot!"

"Barely shot. It doesn't count."

"Barely shot! Alessandro, there's no such thing as *barely shot*!" My voice is rising, hysteria creeping in at the edges. "You got shot because of me. Because we were standing there kissing and someone shot at you, and—"

"Hey." He cups my face, forcing me to look at him. "Breathe. You're okay. We're okay."

"Someone tried to kill you."

"Yes."

"At a Christmas market."

"Yes."

"While we were dancing."

"I know. I'm sorry." He brushes snow from my hair with surprising gentleness. "I should have known better. Should have had more men positioned. Should have—"

"Should have what? Not taken me out? Not tried to have one normal evening?" Tears are burning behind my eyes, but I refuse to let them fall. Not here. Not now. "This is *my* fault. I pushed for this. I wanted normal, and someone almost killed you because of it."

"This is *not* your fault." His voice is fierce. "None of this is your fault. This is Greco. The Russo family. My world bleeding into yours. But Elena, you need to understand, this will keep happening. As long as we're together, you'll be in danger. They'll keep coming after me, and anyone close to me becomes a target."

The words hang between us, heavy with meaning.

He's giving me an out, a chance to walk away before things get worse.

I should take it. Should run as far away from Alessandro De Luca as possible. Should go back to my safe, quiet life, making flower arrangements and drinking coffee in my little apartment, where nobody shoots at me. But when I look at him with snow in his hair, blood on his coat, fear and hope warring in his dark eyes, I know I can't walk away.

"Then I guess we'll need to be more careful," I say.

"Elena—"

"No. I'm not leaving. I'm not running. I'm..." I take a shaky breath. "I'm terrified, and I'm probably going to need therapy after this, and I'm definitely going to have nightmares, but I'm not leaving you."

"You should."

"Probably. But I'm stubborn, remember? When I want something, I don't give up easily." I touch his face, feeling the tension in his jaw. "I want you, Alessandro. Even with the guns and the danger and the people trying to kill you at Christmas markets. I want you."

He closes his eyes as if I've hurt him. "You're going to be the death of me."

"Let's hope not literally."

A choked sound escapes him, half laugh, half sob. When he opens his eyes again, there's something fierce and possessive there that sends heat racing through me despite the cold, the fear, and the chaos.

"Boss, area's clear." A voice crackles in his earpiece. "Shooter's down. We have an exit route."

"Copy." Alessandro stands, pulling me with him. His coat swings open, and I catch a glimpse of the shoulder holster, the gun now tucked away. "We need to go. Police will be here soon, and we don't want to answer their questions."

"But people saw—"

"No one got a clear look at us. Paulo made sure of it." He's already moving, his hand firm around mine. "Come on."

We slip away from the Christmas market through a back alley, leaving behind the screaming, the lights, and the shattered remnants of our *almost-normal* date. A car is waiting, not the Mercedes, something smaller and less conspicuous with Paulo at the wheel.

"Hospital?" Paulo asks as we climb in.

"No. It's barely a scratch. Take us to Elena's."

The drive is silent. Alessandro keeps his arm around me, and I let myself lean into him, suddenly exhausted. My stuffed penguin is somehow still clutched in my other hand, a ridiculous reminder of what this evening was supposed to be.

When we arrive at my apartment, Alessandro walks me upstairs despite my protests about his injury. Inside, he immediately checks the windows, the locks, and the sight lines. He's back to the dangerous man I met in my shop, not the one who danced with me in the snow.

"Alessandro." I catch his hand. "Let me see."

"It's nothing."

"Let. Me. See."

He sighs but shrugs off his coat. The blood has soaked through his Henley at the shoulder, and when he pulls it aside, I see the wound—a deep graze that's still bleeding sluggishly.

"First-aid kit," I say, my voice surprisingly steady. "It's in my bathroom, under the sink. You sit while I get it."

He starts to protest, but I'm already moving. When I return, he's sitting on my couch, looking tired, dangerous, and heartbreakingly human.

"This is going to hurt," I warn as I clean the wound with antiseptic.

"I've had worse."

"That's not comforting."

"It wasn't meant to be."

I work in silence, cleaning and bandaging with hands that only shake a little. When I'm finished, Alessandro catches my wrist, pulling me down to sit beside him.

"Thank you," he says quietly.

"For what? You're the one who got shot protecting me."

"For not running. For staying. For..." he trails off, then tries again. "For seeing *me*. Not the monster. Not the boss. Just... *me*."

The raw honesty in his voice breaks something open in my chest.

"Alessandro De Luca..." I frame his face with my hands. "You are the most infuriating, complicated, dangerous man I've ever met. And I'm completely falling for you."

His eyes go dark. "Elena—"

"I know. It's crazy. It's probably going to end

badly. But I don't care." I lean my forehead against his. "What do we do now?"

"Now?" His arms come around me, pulling me close. "Now we figure out how to keep you safe while I fall completely for you too."

"You're falling for me?"

"*Tesoro*," he murmurs, the Italian endearment soft against my ear. "I've been falling since the moment you smiled at me in your flower shop."

And despite everything—the shooting, the blood, the danger—I smile.

Because this terrifying, beautiful, impossible thing between us?

It's worth fighting for.

Chapter 6

Alessandro

The war room in my downtown office smells like leather, cigar smoke, and violence waiting to happen.

Marco stands at the head of the table, pointing to surveillance photographs of Greco's men and their movements tracked over the past forty-eight hours, spread across the polished mahogany. The sniper from the Christmas market, who is dead, his body dumped in the sound as a message. The underboss who ordered the hit is currently being held in one of our warehouses.

"Three locations," Marco says, tapping the pictures. "Their main drug operation in Georgetown, the gambling house in Belltown, and Greco's personal residence in Madison Park."

"We hit all three," Dante, my head of security,

suggests. He's leaning against the wall, arms crossed. "Simultaneous strikes. Send a message they can't ignore."

"Too flashy," Paulo counters. He's nursing a coffee, looking exhausted. He hasn't slept since the shooting two nights ago. None of us have. "We go in loud like that, the cops will have to respond. Fed attention is the last thing we need right now."

"Fed attention is inevitable after what happened at Pike Place," Luca, my financial guy, points out. "You shot at a civilian Christmas market, boss. It's going to bring heat regardless."

The reminder sits heavy in my chest. Elena, thrown to the ground, covered by my body as bullets flew overhead, her honey-colored eyes wide with terror, while she clutched that ridiculous stuffed penguin, and who should have run screaming but instead bandaged my wound and told me she was falling for me.

"The shooter's identity is scrubbed," Marco says. "No connection to us, no connection to Greco. Far as the cops are concerned, it was random violence. They're treating it as an isolated incident."

"For now," Paulo mutters.

"For now," Marco agrees. "Which means we have a small window to respond before this escalates further. Boss, what's the call?"

All eyes turn to me. This is what they expect— cold calculation, ruthless strategy, and the kind of decisive action that's kept the De Luca family on top for three generations. The Shadow making his move.

"We take the drug operation," my voice comes out flat, emotionless. The voice of a man who's done this a hundred times before. "Tonight. Clean, professional. No bodies left behind, no evidence. We burn their product, destroy their infrastructure, and we make sure every dealer in the city knows what happens when you come after what's fucking mine."

"And Greco himself?" Dante asks.

"Greco gets a message delivered personally. Something he can't misinterpret." The words taste like ash, violence begetting violence, the endless cycle that's defined my entire adult life. "Marco, you handle it. Make it clear, Elena Harper is off-limits. Anyone who looks at her wrong, anyone who so much as breathes near her shop, they answer to me."

Luca raises an eyebrow, but wisely keeps his mouth shut.

"About that," Marco says carefully. "Boss, we need to talk about the girl."

"*No.*"

"You're not even going to hear me out?"

"There's nothing to hear. She's under my protection. That's final."

"Alessandro." Marco drops the formality, which

means he's about to say something he knows won't go over well. "You need to end this. Whatever is happening between you and Elena Harper, end it. *Now*. Before this gets any worse."

The temperature in the room drops ten degrees. Everyone else suddenly finds their phones, their papers, and the ceiling incredibly interesting. No one makes eye contact.

"Care to explain?" Each word is carefully measured.

"Someone tried to kill you at a Christmas market because you were distracted. Because you were too busy playing normal boyfriend to notice the threat." Marco's voice is stern, unyielding. He's the only one who can talk to me like this, the privilege of twenty years of friendship. "Two more seconds of delay and you'd be dead. Because of *her*."

"The threat was neutralized."

"This time. What about next time? Or the time after that?" He leans forward, planting his hands on the table. "You've been sloppy, Alessandro. You're so focused on this woman, you're missing things. Important things. The rest of us see it, even if you don't."

Rage flares hot and immediate. "Watch yourself."

"Someone has to say it. You're compromised. She's a liability—"

"She's *not* a liability, she's..." The words die in my throat because how can Marco possibly understand? How can any of them know what Elena represents? Light in a life that's been nothing but darkness. Honesty in a world built on lies. Something pure and good that has nothing to do with blood, business, or the weight of family expectations crushing down on my shoulders.

"She's what?" Marco challenges. "Your girlfriend? Your weakness? Your Achilles heel waiting to get exploited?"

"*Enough.*" The command cracks through the room like a whip. "Elena stays under protection. You will *not* question this again. Am I clear?"

Marco's jaw works, but he nods. "Crystal."

"Good. The rest of you, be ready to move by twenty-three hundred hours. Paulo, coordinate with the surveillance team. Dante, weapons and backup. Luca, make sure our legal cover is airtight if this goes sideways." Each man nods, filing out one by one until it's only Marco and me left.

"You're making a mistake," he says quietly.

"Maybe. But it's my mistake to make."

"And when they kill her to hurt you? When they use her as leverage? What then?"

The question hits like a physical blow because it's the same thing keeping me awake at night. The same nightmare scenario plays on repeat every time I close my eyes—Elena hurt, bleeding, and paying the price for my selfishness in wanting to keep her close.

"Then every member of the Russo family dies screaming." The words are soft but deadly serious. "Their operations burn. Their families scatter. Their name becomes a cautionary tale whispered in the dark. They will learn what it means to take something from Alessandro De Luca."

Marco studies me for a long moment, then nods slowly. "You love her."

It's not a question.

"Go coordinate the strike," my voice comes out rougher than intended. "We're done here."

He leaves without another word, and the silence that follows is deafening.

Love. The word feels foreign, dangerous. Love makes men weak, makes them vulnerable, makes them do stupid things like bring women to Christmas markets where snipers can take shots at them.

But when Elena smiled at me in the snow, when she kissed me back like nothing else mattered, when she looked at me afterward and said she wasn't leaving—

My phone buzzes.

Elena: *How's your shoulder? Did you change the bandage like I told you to?*

A smile tugs at my mouth despite everything. She's been checking on me constantly, worried about infection, about proper wound care, about things that would never occur to someone in my world where bullets are occupational hazards.

> **Me**: *Yes, doctor. It's fine.*
> **Elena**: *Don't make me come over there and check myself.*
> **Me**: *Is that a threat or a promise?*
> **Elena**: *Now send me a picture proving you changed it.*

The absurdity of it hits me, a mafia boss taking selfies of his bandaged shoulder to appease his worried girlfriend. If the men saw this, they'd never let me live it down.

But instead of being annoyed, warmth spreads through my chest. Someone cares, not about the power, the money, or the fearsome reputation. Someone cares about Alessandro, the man who bleeds, hurts, and apparently needs to be reminded to change his bandages.

Another text arrives while considering my response.

> **Elena**: *Also I made you soup. Nonna's recipe. When can I bring it over?*
> **Me**: *You made me soup?*
> **Elena**: *Don't sound so surprised. I can cook when properly motivated. Answer*

the question. When are you free?

The thought of Elena in my space, my sterile downtown penthouse that's more fortress than home, makes something in my chest constrict. She shouldn't be here. Shouldn't see this side of my life with the maps, weapons, and evidence of exactly what kind of man resides in this building.

But the selfish part—the part that's been starving for something real, something soft—wants nothing more than to see her walk through that door with soup she made with her own hands.

> **Me**: *Tonight's bad. Tomorrow?*
> **Elena**: *Tomorrow works. Your place or mine?*
> **Me**: *Mine. I'll send you the address.*
> **Elena**: *Fancy penthouse, I'm guessing?*
> **Me**: *How did you know?*
> **Elena**: *Because you're you. I bet it's all glass and steel and expensive art. No plants anywhere.*

She knows me too well already.

> **Me**: *There might be one plant.*
> **Elena**. *I'll bring you one tomorrow. Every home needs something living in it.*

Something living. Like her. Like the way she breathes life into every space she occupies, turning a flower shop into magic, my car into a confessional, the Christmas market into something out of a dream.

Before composing a response, a knock interrupts. Dante pokes his head in. "Boss? There's a delivery for you. Guy says it's urgent."

"What kind of delivery?"

"Flowers."

Every muscle in my body goes taut. "From where?"

"No shop name. Guy's a courier service, says he was paid cash to drop it off." Dante's hand rests on his weapon. "You want me to scan it first?"

"Yes. Full sweep. Don't bring it up until you're certain it's clean."

He disappears, and the warmth from Elena's texts evaporates, replaced by cold dread.

Flowers.

An anonymous delivery.

Nothing about this feels right.

Ten minutes later, Dante returns carrying a potted poinsettia. Not the cheerful red and green variety sold at grocery stores, this one is deep crimson, almost black, with leaves that look like they've been dipped in blood.

"Scanned clean," Dante reports, setting it on my desk as if it might explode anyway. "No bugs, no explosives, no biological agents. Just a plant."

"And the courier?"

"Long gone. Paid cash, no description, no way to trace."

Attached to the pot is a small card. My hands are steady as they pluck it free, open it.

Such a pretty flower shop.
Would be a shame if something happened to it.

No signature.

No need for one.

Greco.

The message is clear. They know about Elena. Know about her shop and where to find her if they want to hurt me.

"Dante." My voice is eerily calm despite the rage building beneath the surface like a tsunami. "Move up the timeline. We go tonight. Nineteen hundred hours."

"Boss, that's three hours from now. The men won't be in position—"

"Then they better move fast." Each word is clipped, controlled. "And double the security on Elena's shop. No one gets within a block of Petals & Pines without our people knowing. Am I clear?"

"Crystal. What about her? Should we warn her?"

Should Elena know that she's officially become a target? That someone sent a threatening plant, *a plant, the irony would be funny if it weren't so horrifying*, to make sure the message was received?

"Not yet. She'll panic, and I need her calm until we can neutralize this threat." The lie tastes bitter. This isn't about keeping her calm, but about protecting myself from seeing the fear in her eyes when she realizes exactly what being with me means.

Dante leaves to coordinate, and the poinsettia sits on my desk like an accusation. Its blood-red leaves catch the afternoon light filtering through the floor-to-ceiling windows, beautiful and menacing in equal measure.

My phone buzzes again.

> **Elena**: *You stopped responding. Everything okay?*

No. Nothing is okay. Someone is threatening the one good thing in my life, and all the money, power, and fear my name commands can't change the fact that loving me puts her in danger.

Loving. There's that word again.

> **Me**: *Everything's fine. Just got pulled into a meeting. I'll text you later.*
> **Elena**: *Okay. Stay safe, Shadow.*

Shadow. I told her my nickname for me, and she's

claimed it and says it with affection instead of fear. Like she's tamed the monster, turned something dark into something she can laugh about.

But shadows can't protect anything. They can only watch while the light gets extinguished.

The next three hours pass in a blur of preparation. Weapons checked, teams briefed, exit strategies mapped. Paulo coordinates the surveillance teams. Dante handles the tactical elements. Marco oversees the entire operation with the grim efficiency that's made him invaluable.

The men who'll be staying behind to guard Elena's shop are given explicit instructions— *anything moves toward Petals & Pines, you eliminate the threat first and ask questions never.*

At eighteen hundred hours, Marco appears in my office doorway. "Teams are in position. We're ready when you are."

"Give me five minutes."

He nods and retreats. Alone again, my fingers hover over my phone. One last text to Elena before walking into whatever tonight brings.

> **Me**: *I meant what I said in your apartment. I'm falling for you too.*

The response comes almost immediately.

> **Elena**: *Past tense. I've already fallen.*

Three words. And they rearrange something fundamental in my chest, some piece of armor I've worn for so long, I forgot it was there.

Me: *Then I'll catch you.*
Elena: *Promise?*
Me: *Promise.*

The lie comes easily because what else can be done? Promise her safety in a world where safety doesn't exist? Promise her a future when tomorrow might bring bullets, bombs, or any number of creative ways Greco could choose to hurt me?

All I can offer are lies wrapped in good intentions and the cold comfort that anyone who touches her will die screaming.

It will have to be enough.

Standing, the desk is cleared of everything except the blood-red poinsettia. One more look at Greco's message, at the threat disguised as a gift, then the pot is lifted and carried to the window.

Thirty stories down, the city spreads out like a kingdom. *My kingdom.* Built on blood, fear, and the weight of family legacy. Somewhere down there, Elena is closing her shop, maybe thinking about the soup she made, probably wondering why her mob-boss boyfriend is being cagey about his evening plans.

She deserves better than this.

Better than me.

But selfish men don't give up what they want, and The Shadow has never been anything but selfish.

The window opens, bulletproof glass sliding aside to let in the December cold, and the poinsettia is dropped. It falls, pot and all, thirty stories down to shatter on the concrete below.

A message for a message.

You want to threaten what's mine? Then watch what happens when The Shadow stops playing nice.

"Marco," the call goes out without turning from the window. "Tell the teams we're moving now. And Marco?"

"Yeah, boss?"

"No survivors at the drug house. No mercy. No quarter. They threatened her, so they all burn."

His voice comes back hard with approval. "Understood."

My men file out to their assigned vehicles, their designated targets, their roles in tonight's carefully orchestrated violence. Soon it's just me, alone with the city lights, the cold wind, and the certainty that after tonight, there's no going back.

Greco wanted a war? He'll get one.

But wars have casualties, and the thought of Elena becoming one makes something primitive and vicious uncoil in my chest. Something that wants to tear Greco apart with my bare hands, wants to paint the streets red with anyone who'd dare look at her wrong, wants to burn the entire criminal underworld to ash if that's what it takes to keep her safe.

The phone buzzes one more time.

Elena: *Can't wait to see you tomorrow. Sleep well, Alessandro.*

Sleep. As if sleep were possible with Elena's face in my mind, blood about to be on my hands, and the knowledge that tomorrow, when she shows up with soup, a plant, and that dimpled smile, lies will be told. Pretend nothing happened. Pretend normal. Pretend the man she's falling for isn't currently orchestrating the destruction of an entire criminal operation.

Me: *You too, tesoro. Sweet dreams.*

The phone goes dark. The city glitters below. And Alessandro De Luca, The Shadow, walks into the darkness to do what shadows do best— eliminate threats before they can reach the light.

Because Elena Harper deserves to live in the sunshine, surrounded by flowers, Christmas lights, and the belief that people can be honest and real.

Even if the man she's falling for is neither.

Especially because of that.

The elevator descends.

The war begins.

And somewhere in the distance, a blood-red poinsettia lies shattered on the concrete, a promise and a warning wrapped in broken pottery.

They threatened what's *mine*.

Now they'll learn why people cross the street to avoid The Shadow.

Now they'll learn what happens when you bring winter to a man who's finally found his spring.

Chapter 7

Elena

Morning sunlight streams through the windows of Petals & Pines, catching on the dust motes and turning them into tiny dancers. The coffee maker gurgles in the back room, filling the shop with the rich aroma of dark roast. Christmas music plays softly, Bing Crosby crooning about white Christmases, and everything feels peaceful. Normal.

Which should have been my first warning.

The brick comes through the front window at exactly 8:47 a.m.

Glass explodes inward in a glittering shower, and the sound, *God, the sound* is deafening. Shelves rattle. Vases tip over. My Christmas tree shudders, ornaments swinging wildly.

For a second, shock freezes me in place. Then

training kicks in, not the kind of training normal florists have, but the kind you develop after being shot at in a Christmas market.

Drop. Cover. Assess.

Crouched behind my worktable, heart hammering so hard it might crack my ribs, the shop is surveyed. Glass everywhere. Cold December air is pouring through the jagged hole. And on the floor, amid the scattered flowers and broken pottery, sits a brick wrapped in paper.

No. *No, no, no.*

My hands shake as I reach for the brick and unfold the paper. The message is brief, written in block letters with what appears to be a red marker.

*LEAVE THE SHADOW
OR THE NEXT ONE WON'T MISS!*

The Shadow. Alessandro's nickname. The one whispered in certain circles, the one that makes grown men nervous.

Which means this isn't random vandalism.

This is a message.

For *me.*

About *him.*

The brick slips from numb fingers, clattering to the floor. My shop, my sanctuary, the thing built with bare hands, dreams, and Nonna's memory has been violated. Because of *him.* Because of whatever war he's fighting, whatever enemies he's made.

Because loving *him* makes me a target.

With trembling fingers, I yank my phone from my back pocket and pull up Alessandro's name without thinking. But before I can hit call, the shop door opens.

Correction—what's left of the door opens. The brick took out most of the glass, and now a man steps through, tall, in a dark jacket, cold eyes scanning the destruction with professional interest.

"Elena Harper?" His voice is flat, emotionless.

Every instinct screams danger. "Get out."

"Boss wants to have a conversation." He takes a step forward, glass crunching under his boots.

"I said *get out!*" The pruning shears are grabbed from my worktable, not much of a weapon, but better than nothing. "Now, or I'm calling the police."

"You could do that." Another step. "But then you'd have to explain why someone's threatening you over your boyfriend's business dealings. Lots of uncomfortable questions. Lots of attention on Mr. De Luca. Don't think he'd appreciate that."

He's right. Police mean investigations, investigations mean scrutiny, scrutiny means Alessandro's world gets exposed. And if the movies have taught me anything, exposing a mafia boss doesn't end well for anyone.

"What do you want?"

"Told you. Boss wants to talk." He's maybe ten feet away now, close enough to see the scar running along his jaw. "You can come easily, or we can make it hard. Your choice."

My phone is still clutched in one hand, shears in the other. Fight-or-flight instincts war with each other. Do I run, scream, stab him with the shears, and deal with consequences later? Or go with him?

But before a decision can be made, a voice cuts through the tension like a blade.

"Touch her, and you're dead."

Alessandro.

He's standing in the doorway or what remains of it, dressed in black, his coat open enough to show the gun at his side. His face is absolutely expressionless, but his eyes are filled with murder.

The man in the dark jacket goes very still. "De Luca."

"You have three seconds to walk away." Alessandro's voice is soft, deadly. "One."

"Boss said—"

"Two."

"Look, we're just supposed to deliver a message—"

"Three."

What happens next occurs too fast to process. Alessandro moves, a blur of motion, and suddenly the man is on the ground, Alessandro's knee on his chest, gun pressed to his temple.

"Who sent you?" The question is casual, like he's asking about the weather.

"I don't—"

The gun presses harder. "Wrong answer. *Who. Sent. You.*"

"Greco! Jesus, it was Greco! He just wanted to scare her, make her leave you—"

"Congratulations. You've delivered your message." Alessandro stands, hauling the man up by his collar. "Now you're going to deliver mine. You tell Greco that if anyone, and I mean anyone, comes near this shop again, near Elena again, I will personally dismantle his entire organization. I will take everything he has and burn it to ash. His men, his money, his family. All of it. Am I clear?"

"Y-yes. Crystal."

"Good." Alessandro releases him, and the man stumbles toward the door. "And tell him The Shadow says hello."

The man runs. Literally runs down the street like hell itself is chasing him.

Which leaves Alessandro and me alone in my destroyed shop, glass crunching underfoot, cold air streaming through the broken window, the brick with its threatening message lying on the floor between us.

"Are you hurt?" He's already crossing to me, hands reaching out to check for injuries. "Did he touch you? Did anyone else come in?"

"No, no one else. Just him, the brick, and…" The words tumble out in a rush. "Alessandro, what the hell is happening? Who was that? What did he mean about leaving you?"

His hands still on my arms. "We should talk."

"We're past talking! Someone just threw a brick through my window and threatened me because of *you*!" The volume rises despite attempts to stay calm. "And you show up like some kind of avenging angel with a gun and death threats, and how did you even get here so fast?"

"I had men watching the shop."

"You had—" The words die in my throat. "You've been watching me?"

"Protecting you. There's a difference."

"Is there? Because from where I'm standing, it feels an awful lot like surveillance." Hands rake through her hair, leaving it disheveled. "God, I knew you were dangerous. I knew you weren't just an importer. But this? Men with guns, threats, people watching my shop?"

"Elena—"

"Don't. Just… don't." Distance is needed, space to think without those dark eyes making everything fuzzy, but there's nowhere to go in the small shop. Glass is everywhere, and the cold air keeps pouring through the broken window like a physical reminder that nothing is safe anymore.

Alessandro's jaw works. "Pack a bag."

"Excuse me?"

"Pack a bag. You're staying with me until this is resolved."

"Like hell I am!"

"This isn't a request." His voice drops into that tone, the one that probably makes his men scramble to obey. "Greco knows where you live, where you work. He's already made one move. He'll make another."

"So what? Am I supposed to abandon my shop? My life? Move in with you because some mobster has a grudge?"

"*Yes.*"

The simplicity of it, the absolute certainty in that one word, is infuriating. "You can't just order me around, Alessandro."

"I can when it's your safety at stake." He moves closer, and despite everything, my traitorous body responds to his proximity. "Please. I know you're angry. You have every right to be. But right now, I need you somewhere I can protect you. Somewhere with security and backup and no giant windows that bricks can come through."

"For how long?"

"As long as it takes."

"That's not an answer."

"It's the only answer I have." His hand comes up to cup my cheek, thumb brushing across the bone. "I can't, Elena, if something happened to you because of me, I wouldn't survive it."

The raw honesty in his voice cracks something in my chest. Here stands a man who probably kills people for a living, who carries a gun like it's a wallet, who just threatened to dismantle an entire organization, and he's looking at me like I'm the most fragile, precious thing in the world.

"One condition," the words come out softer than intended.

"Anything."

"You tell me *everything*. No more secrets, no more lies. I want to know *exactly* what I'm dealing with."

He hesitates, and for a moment, the possibility exists he'll refuse. Then, "Everything. I promise."

"Okay." A shaky breath escapes. "Okay. Let me get some things."

Alessandro's penthouse is exactly what I predicted—all glass, steel, and expensive minimalist furniture that looks like it's never been used. Floor-to-ceiling windows offer panoramic views of the city, and the kitchen gleams with stainless steel appliances. The living room could fit my entire apartment twice over.

And there's not a plant in sight.

"Guest room is down the hall," Alessandro says, setting down the hastily packed overnight bag. "En suite bathroom, walk-in closet. Make yourself at home."

"This place doesn't look like anyone's ever made themselves at home here." The observation comes out before it can be stopped.

The corner of his mouth twitches. "That obvious?"

"It looks like a hotel suite. Beautiful, but completely impersonal." A hand waves at the generic modern art on the walls, the lack of photographs, the absolute absence of anything that indicates a human being actually lives here. "Do you even sleep here?"

"Sometimes. When I'm not at the office." He shrugs off his coat, and the gun holster is suddenly very visible against his black shirt. "I'm not here much."

"Because you're too busy running your criminal empire?"

The words come out more bitter than intended, and Alessandro's expression shutters. "I told you I'd explain everything. Let me get the window situation handled at your shop first, then we'll talk."

"Fine. But Alessandro?" He turns back at the

door. "Thank you. For coming so fast. For being there."

Something soft crosses his face. "Always, *tesoro*."

He leaves to make phone calls, and the guest room becomes my temporary sanctuary. It's as impersonal as the rest of the penthouse, with neutral colors, expensive linens, and a bed big enough for three people. I unpack my overnight bag with hands that won't quite stop shaking.

Someone threatened me.

Threw a brick through my window because of Alessandro.

The smart thing would be to leave. Pack up, get out, maybe even leave Seattle entirely until this blows over.

But when Alessandro looked at me in the shop, when he said he wouldn't survive something happening to me, every rational thought dissolved like sugar in hot coffee.

Clearly, falling in love with a mobster has destroyed all common sense.

Falling in love. The thought should terrify me more than it does.

The shower in the en-suite bathroom is probably the fanciest thing ever experienced. It has a rainfall head, multiple jets, and controls that look like they belong on a spaceship. The hot water feels like heaven, washing away the adrenaline, fear, and glass dust.

When emerging twenty minutes later in clean jeans and a soft sweater, voices drift from the main room. Alessandro and someone else, a male with a familiar voice.

"… pushing too hard, too fast," the other voice says. "You need to think strategically—"

"I am thinking strategically, Marco. Strategically keeping Elena alive."

"By what, moving her into your penthouse? Making her an even bigger target?"

Feet freeze in the hallway. Eavesdropping is wrong. Everyone knows this. But they're talking about me, which feels like justification enough.

"She's safer here than at her apartment with no security." Alessandro sounds tired. "What would you have me do? Leave her there to wait for the next brick? Or worse?"

"I'd have you end this before it gets her *killed*!" Marco's voice rises. "You're not thinking clearly. You're compromised, and when you're compromised, people die."

"Marco—"

"No, you need to hear this. This woman, Elena, has made you soft. Sloppy. Three weeks ago, you would've seen Greco's move coming. You would've had countermeasures in place. But instead, you're playing house and buying flowers and getting shot at Christmas markets because you're too distracted to—"

"*Enough.*" The word cracks like a whip. "Elena stays. The discussion is over."

Silence falls, heavy and tense. Then Marco sighs. "You're falling in love with her."

"That's none of your concern."

"It's absolutely my concern when it affects your judgment. Alessandro, listen to me, you cannot protect her and fight this war at the same time. Eventually, you'll have to choose."

"Then I choose *her.*"

The words hang in the air, and something warm and terrifying unfurls in my chest. He chooses me over his business, his men's advice, and whatever strategic considerations Marco is worried about.

He chooses *me.*

"I hope you don't regret that," Marco says quietly. "I really do."

Footsteps approach the hallway, which means it's time to either announce my presence or get caught eavesdropping. The decision is made when I step into the living room, as if nothing had been heard.

"Oh, sorry. Didn't mean to interrupt."

Marco turns, and up close, he's younger than I expected, maybe early thirties, handsome in a sharp-featured way, with eyes that assess and categorize in seconds. "Elena. We haven't been formally introduced. Marco Rinaldi, Alessandro's second."

"Second-in-command," Alessandro clarifies. "He runs operations when I'm... occupied."

"Nice to meet you." The words come out stiff, formal. Hard to be friendly with someone who wants Alessandro to dump me for strategic purposes.

Marco's eyes flick between us, and something like resignation crosses his face. "I should go. Boss, think about what I said."

"I have. The answer's still *no*."

"Figured as much." Marco nods at me. "Ms. Harper. Stay safe."

Then he's gone, leaving Alessandro and me alone in the cavernous penthouse with the weight of overheard conversations between us.

"How much did you hear?" Alessandro asks.

"Enough." No point in lying. "He's right, you know. About me being a distraction."

"He's wrong." Alessandro crosses to where I'm standing, and suddenly the huge space feels very small. "You're not a distraction. You're the only thing keeping me sane right now."

"Alessandro—"

"You wanted the truth. Here it is." He's close enough now that his cologne, something dark and expensive, fills my senses. "Yes, I run criminal operations in Seattle. Yes, I've killed people. Yes, being with me puts you in danger. But you also make me want to be better than what I am. Make

118

me remember there's more to life than territory and profit margins and body counts."

His hand comes up to cup my face, and despite everything—the danger, the fear, Marco's warnings—I lean into his touch.

"I'm terrified," the admission comes out barely above a whisper. "Of this, of you, of what loving you might cost."

"You should be."

"But I can't seem to stop. Can't seem to walk away." My hand covers his, holding it against my cheek. "What does that make me?"

"*Mine*," he says, and then his mouth is on mine.

The kiss is different from the others. It's desperate, claiming, as if he's trying to pour every emotion he can't articulate into this connection. Hands tangle in his hair, my body presses against his, and nothing else exists except this moment, this man, this impossible thing between us.

Alessandro walks me backward until my spine hits the cold glass of the window. His hands slide under my sweater, fingers splaying across bare skin, and heat floods through my body.

"Tell me to stop," he murmurs against my mouth. "Tell me this is moving too fast."

"Don't stop." The words come out breathy, desperate. "Please... *don't stop*."

He groans, a sound that goes straight through me, and his mouth moves to my neck, his teeth grazing sensitive skin. One hand slides higher under my sweater, and when his thumb brushes the underside of my breast through my bra, a sound escapes that definitely qualifies as a moan.

"Cristo," he mutters. "Elena—"

"Bedroom." I can barely form words. "We should... bedroom."

But even as the suggestion is made, Alessandro pulls back. His breathing is ragged, his hair messed from my fingers, his eyes almost black with desire, and he's shaking his head.

"We can't."

The words are like a cold water slap. "What?"

"We can't do this. Not yet. Not like this." He steps back, putting distance between us, and the loss of his warmth is actually painful.

"Alessandro, I'm a grown woman. I know what I want—"

"I know. Believe me, I know." His hand rakes through his hair. "But you just found out about my world. You're staying here because you're in danger. Starting this now when everything is chaos and fear and adrenaline, that's not how I want this to happen." Alessandro shakes his head and takes another step back.

"How *you* want it to happen? What about what *I* want?"

"What you want is influenced by proximity, danger, and your body's response to stress." His voice is gentle but firm. "When we do this, and *we will*, I want you to have no doubts. No questions. I want you to choose me when you're not running from someone else's threats."

The logic is sound.

Infuriating, but sound.

"I hate that you're being reasonable right now." The complaint comes out in a sulky tone.

"I hate it too." His smile is pained. "Trust me, turning you down is the hardest thing I've done in years."

"Good. Suffer." But there's no real heat in my words.

He laughs, the sound surprised and genuine. "You're something else, you know that?"

"So, I've been told." A step forward, then another, until we're close again. Not touching, but close enough to feel his body heat. "But Alessandro? When this is over, when Greco is handled, and I've had time to process everything, and I choose you anyway, all bets are off."

His eyes darken. "Is that a threat?"

"It's a promise."

"I'm going to hold you to that."

"Good."

We stand there, suspended in tension, want, and the sweet torture of almost. Outside, the city looks vast. Inside, awareness crackles between us like electricity.

"I should let you rest," Alessandro finally says. "It's been a long day."

"Will you tell me? Everything? Like you promised?"

"Tomorrow. Over breakfast. I'll lay it all out, the family, the business, what we're up against." His hand reaches out, tucking a strand of damp hair behind my ear. "But now, rest. You're safe here. I promise."

"Will you be here? Or do you have... business?"

"I'll be here. Down the hall in my room. If you need anything..."

"I know where to find you."

Something passes between us, understanding, maybe? Or acknowledgment of what almost happened, what still might happen, what we're both desperately trying to resist.

"Go rest, Elena."

I nod, he leaves, and the penthouse suddenly feels even more enormous. The guest room beckons, but sleep seems impossible. Too much adrenaline, fear, and want are still humming through my veins.

The bed is comfortable, though. The sheets are expensive and soft.

Hours later, city lights filter through the windows, casting shadows across the ceiling.

Somewhere down the hall, Alessandro is most likely not sleeping either, probably thinking about the same almost-kiss, the same almost-more, the same impossible situation that's drawing us together despite every logical reason to stay apart.

Tomorrow brings explanations. Truth. The full picture of what loving Alessandro De Luca actually means.

But tonight, in this borrowed room in this sterile penthouse, the only thing crystal clear is this— running would be smarter.

Safer.

But when his hands were on my skin, when his mouth was on mine, when he looked at me like I was the only real thing in his violent world, safety stopped mattering.

Chapter 8

Alessandro

Sleep refuses to come.

The penthouse is silent except for the ambient hum of the city thirty floors below. Every shadow could be a threat. Every creak of settling steel and glass sends adrenaline spiking. Old habits die hard, and the habit of sleeping with one eye open has kept me alive for fifteen years.

That, and the knowledge that Elena is down the hall in the guest room, vulnerable, trusting, and entirely unprepared for the kind of violence that follows men like me.

The clock on the nightstand reads 2:47 a.m. when soft footsteps pad down the hallway. Every muscle tenses, my hand instinctively reaching for the gun on the nightstand before recognition kicks in.

Those footsteps are too light, too hesitant.

Not a threat.

Elena.

The bedroom door opens slowly, a sliver of hallway light cutting through the darkness. She's silhouetted in the doorway, small, uncertain, wearing what looks like an oversized T-shirt that hits mid-thigh.

"Alessandro?" Her voice is barely a whisper. "Are you awake?"

Sitting up triggers the motion sensor on the bedside lamp, casting soft light across the room. "What's wrong? Did something happen?"

"No, nothing happened. I just..." She wraps her arms around herself. "I couldn't sleep. Every time I close my eyes, I see that brick coming through the window. Or that man in my shop. Or..." Her breath hitches. "Is it okay if I stay here? Just for a little while?"

Every rational thought screams this is a *terrible* idea. Elena in the guest room is manageable. Elena in this room, in a T-shirt, looking vulnerable, beautiful, and completely off-limits, that's a special kind of torture.

"Of course." The words come out rougher than intended. "Come here."

She crosses to the bed, and up close, the T-shirt is revealed to be one of mine. She must have found it in the guest room closet. It swallows her frame, the collar slipping off one shoulder, and the sight of her wearing something of mine does something primal to my chest.

"Which side do you want?" The question is practical, normal, as if sharing a bed with the woman who is slowly unraveling every defense mechanism is completely fine.

"I don't care. Whichever you're not using."

"Right side, then." The covers are pulled back, an invitation and a test of self-control. Elena climbs in, keeping a careful distance. The bed is king-size, plenty of room for two people to sleep without touching. But somehow, even with a foot of space between us, her presence is overwhelming—the scent of her shampoo, the sound of her breathing, the warmth radiating from her skin.

"Thank you," she says quietly. "For letting me stay. For not... judging."

"There's nothing to judge. After what you went through today, anyone would be shaken."

"You're not shaken."

"Years of practice."

She turns on her side to face me, head propped on one hand. In the dim light, her honey-colored eyes are dark, searching. "How many years?"

"Too many to count."

"That's not an answer."

"No, it's not." Rolling onto my side mirrors her position, facing her across the pillow barrier between us. "But it's the truth. When you grow up in this life, you learn early that showing fear gets you killed. You learn to bury it. To function despite it."

"That sounds exhausting."

"It is."

Her hand reaches out, tentative, and settles on the pillow between us. Not touching, but close enough that moving an inch would bridge the gap. "Do you ever get tired of it? The constant vigilance? The violence?"

Every single day. "Sometimes."

"What would you do if you could just walk away?"

The question catches me off guard. No one has ever asked what Alessandro De Luca would do if he weren't The Shadow. What dreams died when my father's blood soaked into marble floors, and a sixteen-year-old boy had to become a man overnight.

"I don't know," the admission comes slowly. "Maybe something quiet. Normal. Something that doesn't require checking for exits in every room or sleeping with a gun under my pillow."

Her eyes flick to the nightstand where the weapon rests. "Is that why you couldn't sleep? Because you were on guard?"

"Partly. Also, because you're under this roof, which means ensuring nothing happens to you."

"Alessandro, you can't stay awake all night protecting me."

"Watch me."

She studies my face for a long moment, then makes a decision. The space between us closes as she moves across the invisible barrier, tucking herself against my chest with a boldness that steals my breath.

"What are you doing?" The question comes out strained.

"If you're going to stay awake guarding me anyway, I might as well be comfortable." Her head rests on my shoulder, one arm draping across my stomach. "This okay?"

Okay doesn't begin to cover it. She's warm, soft, and fits against me like she was designed for this exact purpose. Every nerve ending is suddenly hyperaware with her breath on my neck, her leg brushing against mine, the weight of her body pressed to my side.

"Elena—"

"Please don't push me away. Not tonight." Her voice is small, vulnerable. "I just need to know I'm safe. We're safe. Even if it's an illusion."

My arms wrap around her before conscious thought intervenes, one hand settling on her hip, the other threading through her hair. "You're safe. I promise."

She sighs, tension melting from her frame.

"Thank you."

"For what?"

"For being you. Dangerous and protective and completely contradictory." Her fingers trace absent patterns on my chest through the thin fabric of my sleep shirt. "Marco's right, you know. You should probably send me away. Put me on a plane to somewhere safe until this is over."

"Marco worries too much."

"Does he? Or does he see something you're too close to see?"

The question deserves honesty. "He sees that caring about you makes me vulnerable. Love is a weakness in our world."

Her hand stills on my chest. "Love?"

The word slipped out without permission, but there's no taking it back now. "Love. Affection. Whatever term makes it less terrifying."

"None of them make it less terrifying." She tilts her head back to look at me, and the vulnerability in her eyes mirrors what's probably showing in mine. "But I don't think I'd change it even if I could."

"You should want to change it. Run far away from me and this whole mess."

"Probably. But I've never been good at doing what I should." Her hand resumes its pattern-tracing, now moving up to my collarbone, my neck. "Tell me something true. Something you've never told anyone else."

The request is dangerous. Truth is currency in my world, something to be guarded and rationed. But with Elena warm against me, her touch sending electricity through my skin, my defenses crumble.

"Sometimes I dream about a different life. One where I'm just Alessandro, not The Shadow. Where I can walk into a flower shop and buy roses without calculating threat assessments. Where the woman I care about doesn't need armed guards and bulletproof glass." The confession comes out rough. "But then I wake up, and this is still my reality. This is all I know how to be."

"What if you could learn to be something else?"

"Men like me don't get redemption arcs, *tesoro*. We get prison or death, and if we're lucky, we get to choose which."

She's quiet for a moment, processing. "I don't believe that. I think people can change if they want to badly enough."

"And what would I change into? A florist?" The attempt at humor falls flat.

"Why not? You obviously have good taste in flowers. And you know all about thorns and danger and things that are beautiful but can hurt you." Her fingers trace the line of my jaw. "Sounds perfect."

Despite everything, the danger, the exhaustion, the impossible situation, a laugh escapes. "A mob boss turned florist. That's a new one."

"See? You're already thinking about possibilities."

"I'm thinking you're dangerously optimistic."

"Someone has to be. You're pessimistic enough for both of us." She yawns, the sound muffled against my chest. "Stay with me? Until I fall asleep?"

"I'm not going anywhere."

Her breathing gradually evens out, her body growing heavy with sleep. But true to form, vigilance remains. Every sound is cataloged, every shadow assessed. The gun on the nightstand is within easy reach. The security system monitors every entry point.

But somewhere between checking the cameras and listening for threats, exhaustion finally wins. The last conscious thought is of Elena's warmth, her trust, and the way she chose to seek safety in the arms of the most dangerous man she knows.

And then, for the first time in months, sleep comes, deep, dreamless, and surprisingly peaceful.

Sunlight streams through floor-to-ceiling windows, providing the wake-up call I need. For a disoriented moment, the situation doesn't register. Why is there weight on my chest? Why does everything smell like vanilla and flowers?

Then memory returns. *Elena.* In my bed. Still tucked against my side as if she belongs there.

Sometime during the night, positions shifted. She's half on top of me now, one leg thrown over mine, her face pressed into the curve of my neck. My arms are wrapped around her possessively, one hand tangled in her hair, the other resting on the small of her back where the T-shirt has ridden up to reveal warm, soft skin.

This is dangerous.

This is playing with fire.

This is—

She stirs, making a slight sound of contentment, and any thought of extricating myself evaporates. When her eyes flutter open and meet mine, still hazy with sleep, something in my chest cracks wide open.

"Morning," she mumbles, not moving. "You actually slept."

"Apparently."

"Good. You needed it." She stretches, catlike, and the movement presses her body closer against mine. Heat floods through me, and she must feel the evidence of exactly what her proximity is doing because her eyes widen slightly. "Oh."

"Sorry. Morning biology. Can't exactly control it."

"Don't apologize." Her voice drops lower, intimate. "It's... flattering."

"Elena." Her name comes out as a warning.

"Alessandro." She mirrors the tone, teasing.

"We agreed—"

"You agreed. I distinctly remember expressing a different opinion." Her hand slides up my chest, over my shoulder, fingers threading through my hair. "But you're right. We should get up. You promised me breakfast and explanations."

The reminder of what today holds, the conversation that can't be avoided any longer, help dampen some of the heat. "Right. Breakfast."

Neither of us moves.

"Elena."

"I know, I know. We're getting up." But instead of pulling away, she leans in and presses a kiss to my jaw. Then another, lower, at the corner of my mouth. "Just one more minute."

Self-control has limits, and mine are currently being tested beyond reason. Hands grip her hips, prepared to set her away, but she chooses that moment to shift her weight, and suddenly, she's straddling me, the T-shirt riding up to reveal bare thighs and Cristo, matching black lace underneath.

"You're trying to kill me." The accusation comes out strained.

"Maybe a little." Her smile is wicked. "Is it working?"

"Very effectively."

She leans down, hair falling around us like a curtain, mouth hovering just above mine. "Then my work here is done."

And then she's gone, scrambling off the bed with a laugh, leaving me hard, frustrated, and completely at her mercy.

"You're evil." The observation is called after her retreating form.

"You like it!" Comes the response from the hallway.

The truth is, 'like' doesn't begin to cover what Elena makes me feel. But admitting that to her or to myself opens doors better left closed.

Thirty minutes later, the kitchen has been transformed into something almost domestic. Eggs are being scrambled on the stove. Coffee percolates. Elena sits at the kitchen island in jeans and a sweater, hair still damp from her shower, watching with amusement as breakfast is prepared.

"You can cook," she observes.

"Basic survival skill."

"Most men in your position would have a chef."

"Most men in my position don't know how to be alone with their thoughts." I plate the eggs, add toast, and pour Elena a coffee. "Here."

She takes the plate with a smile that does things to my chest. "Thank you. This looks great."

We eat in comfortable silence for a few minutes.

But eventually, the reprieve ends.

"So," Elena says, setting down her fork. "You promised me the truth. All of it."

"Not all of it. Some things are better left unknown."

"Alessandro..."

"But I'll tell you what I can." I set the coffee cup down and fold my hands on the counter. Where to even begin? "My family, the De Lucas, we've controlled organized crime in Seattle for three generations. My grandfather started it, my father expanded it, and now it's mine."

"What exactly does 'organized crime' mean?"

"Protection rackets. Gambling operations. Some drug trafficking, though I'm trying to phase that out. Money laundering. The occasional... removal of obstacles."

Her eyes widen. "Removal of obstacles. You mean murder."

"Yes."

She absorbs this, and watching her process the reality of what has been done and what continues to be done is harder than any interrogation. "How many people have you killed?"

"Does the number matter?"

"Yes. No. I don't know." She rakes a hand through her hair. "I'm trying to reconcile the man who makes me breakfast with the man who admits to murder like it's a business meeting."

"They're the same person, Elena. That's what you need to understand. I'm not two separate people... one good, one bad. I'm just this. Violence and tenderness, protection and danger. All of it wrapped up in one very complicated package."

"And Greco? The Russo family? What do they want?"

"My territory. My operations. Everything I've built." The explanation continues, laying out the territorial disputes, the escalating violence, and the reasons why a Christmas market became a battlefield. "Greco thinks he can take what's mine through intimidation and force. He's wrong."

"And me? Where do I fit into all this?"

"You don't. You shouldn't." The truth is bitter. "You're an innocent caught in the crossfire because I was selfish enough to want something normal. Something pure."

"Stop that." Her hand reaches across the counter, finding mine. "Stop acting like you're some irredeemable monster. You're a man who made choices in impossible circumstances. That doesn't make you evil."

"Doesn't make me good either."

"No, but it makes you human." She squeezes my hand. "And the human part, the part that buys flowers for his mother and dances in the snow and holds me when I'm scared, that's the part I'm choosing to believe in."

"You shouldn't."

"Too late. Already did." She stands, moving around the island to stand between my knees. "So here's what's going to happen. You're going to stop trying to scare me away. I'm going to stay here until this Greco situation is resolved. And we're both going to stop pretending this thing between us isn't exactly what it feels like."

"And what does it feel like?" The question is dangerous, but it needs asking.

"Like falling. Like fire. Like something inevitable and terrifying and completely worth the risk." Her hands frame my face, forcing eye contact. "I'm not going anywhere, Alessandro. You might as well stop fighting it."

"I hurt people, Elena. I destroy lives. That's what I do."

"Maybe. But you also protect what's yours with everything you have. You care about your men. You tried to push me away to keep me safe." Her thumb brushes across my cheekbone. "That's not a monster. That's a man who's been forced to be hard because the world he lives in demands it."

The words crack something open, some carefully maintained wall that's kept emotions at bay for years. Arms wrap around her waist, pulling her closer, and for a moment, vulnerability is allowed, just this once, only with her.

"I don't know how to do this," the confession is

muffled against her sweater. "How to be what you need and what my world demands."

"Then we'll figure it out together." Her fingers thread through my hair, gentle and grounding. "But Alessandro? You need to let me in. Really in. Not just the sanitized version you think I can handle."

"You say that now. But when you see what I'm really capable of—"

"Then I'll decide if I can live with it. But you don't get to make that choice for me." She pulls back just enough to meet my eyes. "Deal?"

Looking at her, this stubborn, brave, impossibly optimistic woman who's choosing danger over safety, me over common sense, my only possible response is truth.

"Deal."

She smiles, and the room suddenly feels brighter. "Good. Now, what's the plan? How do we handle Greco?"

"We don't handle anything. I handle it while you stay here, safe, behind reinforced steel and armed guards."

"Alessandro—"

"This is non-negotiable, Elena. You're not going anywhere near this situation." The command comes out sharper than intended. "You'll stay here, where I can protect you, until Greco is no longer a threat."

Her eyes narrow. "I'm just supposed to sit here

like some damsel in distress while you go off and do... what? Fight some mob war?"

"Essentially, yes."

"And how long is that going to take?"

"As long as it takes."

"That's not an answer!"

"It's the only answer I have." Standing puts us at eye level, and the frustration in her expression mirrors what's churning in my gut. "I know you want to be involved. I know you want to help. But the best way you can help is by staying safe so I can focus on neutralizing the threat instead of worrying about you."

"I'm not a child, Alessandro. You can't just lock me in a tower—"

"I can, and I will if it means keeping you alive." The words come out hard, final. "This isn't up for discussion."

Her jaw sets in that stubborn line that means she's gearing up for an argument. But then something shifts in her expression, calculation replacing irritation.

"Okay," she says slowly. "I'll stay here. On one condition."

Suspicion immediately rises. "What condition?"

"You teach me."

"Teach you what?"

"How to protect myself. Basic self-defense. How to shoot a gun. Whatever you think I need to know to survive in your world." Her chin lifts, defiant. "If I'm going to be a target, I should at least know how to defend myself. Unless you disagree?"

The logic is sound, which is exactly the problem. Teaching Elena to handle weapons, to fight, to think like someone in this life, it's another step toward pulling her deeper into darkness.

But she's right. If Greco is already making moves, if other families might see her as leverage, she needs skills beyond flower arranging and stubborn optimism.

"Fine. But you follow my instructions exactly. No improvising, no arguing, no doing something reckless because you think you know better."

"I can agree to that."

"And you stay in this penthouse except for training. No going back to your shop, no visiting friends, no anything without explicit approval from me or my security team."

Her expression tightens, but she nods. "Agreed."

"And Elena?" A step closer eliminates the space between us, and her breath catches. "When this is over, when Greco is handled, and you're safe again, we're going to have a very long conversation about boundaries and risk assessment and why arguing with me in life-or-death situations is a terrible idea."

"Is that a threat?" But there's heat in her eyes now, awareness sparking between us.

"It's a promise."

"Good." Her hands slide up my chest, over my shoulders, linking behind my neck. "I'll hold you to it."

Then she's kissing me, fierce, demanding, and completely inappropriate for a conversation about mortal danger. But rational thought evaporates the moment her mouth meets mine, her body presses against mine, and she makes that slight sound in the back of her throat that drives me absolutely insane.

We break apart, breathing hard, and the look she gives me is part challenge, part invitation, making it clear exactly what she wants.

And maybe, just maybe, after all the violence, darkness, and careful control, letting go with this one person might not be the worst idea.

But not yet. Not until she's seen the full extent of what loving The Shadow truly means.

"Later," the promise is rough against her lips. "When you've had time to really understand what you're choosing. When there's no doubt."

"I don't have doubts now."

"You will. And when they come, I want you to work through them with full information." I place a soft and chaste kiss on her forehead, the opposite of what both of us want. "Trust me on this."

Elena sighs but steps back. "You're incredibly frustrating, you know that?"

"So, I've been told."

"But also…" She bites her lip, and the vulnerability in her eyes stops my heart. "Also kind of amazing in a terrifying, complicated, probably-going-to-give-me-a-heart-attack kind of way."

"I'll take it."

Her smile could light the entire city. "Good. Because you're stuck with me now."

"Are you threatening me?"

"You can count on it."

And standing there in my sterile penthouse kitchen with morning light streaming through bulletproof glass and a woman who shouldn't want anything to do with me smiling like I'm worth loving, for the first time in fifteen years, hope feels like something more than a liability.

It feels like a possibility.

Even if that possibility comes wrapped in danger, blood, and the certainty that the coming days will test everything we think we know about love, loyalty, and how far someone will go to protect what's theirs.

But that's a problem for later.

Right now, Elena is in my kitchen, looking at me like I'm worth the risk.

Chapter 9

Elena

Three days of living in Alessandro's penthouse feel like three years.

Not because it's unpleasant, it's the opposite. The space is beautiful, the bed is comfortable, and the view is spectacular. Alessandro's chef delivers meals that should probably be illegal. The security team is invisible but ever-present.

But Alessandro himself? He's become a ghost.

He leaves early for 'business,' and returns late smelling like danger and exhaustion. He sits across from me at dinner, making polite conversation as though we're strangers instead of two people who have kissed like the world is ending. He stays carefully, deliberately distant in a way that's starting to drive me insane.

The self-defense training is the only time he

touches me, and even then, it's clinical and professional. His hands correct my stance, adjust my grip on the gun, demonstrate how to break free from various holds, all of it done with the detached efficiency of someone teaching a skill set, not someone who had me straddling him in bed three mornings ago.

It's maddening.

"Again." Alessandro's voice cuts through my frustration. We're in the building's private gym, all mirrors, equipment, and mats that smell like rubber and sweat. "Someone grabs you from behind. What do you do?"

"Step back, disrupt their balance, elbow to the ribs, heel to instep, turn and strike." The movements are executed as taught, mechanical and precise.

"Better. But you're telegraphing the elbow. The element of surprise is crucial." He demonstrates, moving behind me to show the proper form. His chest presses against my back, his arms coming around to position mine correctly. "See? Smooth, no warning. Then…" He guides the motion, slow and controlled. "Impact here causes maximum pain with minimum effort."

His breath is warm on my neck. Solid presence surrounds me. This close, his cologne mingles with something uniquely him and soap, and it makes my brain short-circuit.

"Elena." His voice is rough. "Are you paying attention?"

"Yes." The lie comes out breathy. "Totally paying attention. Elbows. Ribs. Got it."

He steps back abruptly, putting distance between us. "Take five. You're distracted."

Distracted is putting it mildly. Sexually frustrated is more accurate. Slowly going insane from want might be the most honest description.

I grab the water bottle with more force than necessary. "When do we work on shooting again?"

"Tomorrow, maybe. Depends on my schedule."

"Your mysterious, important schedule that you can't tell me about."

"Yes."

"Because you're off doing dangerous mob things."

"Yes."

"Things that might get you killed."

"Possibly." He doesn't even look up from his phone, scrolling through what's probably emails about territorial disputes and strategic violence.

"And I'm just supposed to sit here and wait? Not knowing if you're safe? Not knowing if..." The words catch in my throat. "Not knowing if you're coming back?"

That gets his attention. He sets the phone down, dark eyes finding mine across the gym. "I always come back."

"You can't promise that."

"No, but I can promise I'll do everything in my power to make sure I do." He stands, crossing to where the water bottles sit, takes one, drinks, watching me over the rim like he's trying to figure out a puzzle. "This is what my life looks like, Elena. Late nights, dangerous situations, uncertainty. If you can't handle it—"

"*Don't.*" The word comes out sharp. "Don't use my worry as an excuse to push me away. Don't act like caring about whether you live or die means I'm not cut out for this."

"I'm not."

"You are. You've been doing it for three days." Stepping closer eliminates some of the careful distance he maintains. "You barely look at me. You don't touch me unless it's training. You leave before I wake up and come back after I'm asleep. If you've changed your mind about us, just say it. Don't make me guess."

His jaw works. "I haven't changed my mind."

"Then what is this?" I throw my hands around. "Why are you avoiding me?"

"I'm trying to protect you."

"From what? Greco? Your enemies? Because news flash, Alessandro, I'm already in danger. I'm already a target. Avoiding me doesn't change that."

"I'm trying to protect you from me," he says quietly, and something raw flashes across his face.

"From what I want to do to you. From how dark the wanting gets when you're close."

Oh.

Oh.

Heat floods through me, pooling low in my belly. "What if I want that too?"

"You don't know what you're asking for."

"Then show me." Another step closer, and now we're in each other's space, breathing the same air. "Stop treating me like I'm made of glass. Stop hiding whatever you think will scare me away."

"*Elena.*" My name is a warning.

"*Alessandro.*" His name is a challenge.

Something shifts in his expression, his control cracks, the careful mask slips. His hand comes up to cup my face, his thumb brushing across my bottom lip with a possessiveness that sends shivers down my spine.

"You have no idea what you do to me," he murmurs. "How much I want you. How hard it is to maintain any semblance of control when you're in my space, wearing my clothes, looking at me like I'm something other than a monster."

"You're not a monster."

"Yes, I am. And when I finally give in, when I stop fighting this, you're going to see exactly what kind of monster wants you."

The words should probably terrify me. Instead, they light something primal and hungry in my core.

"Try me."

His eyes go almost black. "You're playing with fire, *tesoro*."

"Maybe I like the burn."

For one suspended moment, neither of us moves. Then his control shatters.

He kisses me like he's drowning, and I'm oxygen, desperate, consuming, nothing gentle about it. One hand tangles in my hair, tilting my head back to deepen the angle. The other grips my hip, pulling me flush against him so every hard plane of his body presses against mine.

This isn't the sweet kiss under Christmas lights. This isn't the restrained affection of someone holding back. This is raw need, barely leashed desire, and the promise of exactly how dark his wanting can get.

"Alessandro," his name comes out as a gasp when his mouth moves to my neck, teeth grazing sensitive skin. "We're in the gym."

"Don't care." His hand slides under my tank top, splaying across bare skin. "Been trying to be good. Trying to give you space. But Cristo, Elena, you make it impossible."

"Good. Be impossible with me." Fingers tangle in his hair, holding him close as his mouth does devastating things to my neck. "Stop holding back."

He groans against my skin, and then he's moving, backing me up until my spine hits the mirrored wall. The cold glass contrasts sharply with the heat of his body, and when his thigh slides between my legs, pressing exactly where the ache has been building for days, a moan escapes that echoes in the empty gym.

"That sound," he mutters. "I want to hear you make that sound again. And again. Until it's the only thing I can remember."

His thigh presses harder, and pleasure spikes through me. "Alessandro..."

"Tell me to stop." His hand slides higher under my shirt, fingers tracing the edge of my sports bra. "Tell me you don't want this."

"I can't." Because it would be a lie. Because every nerve ending is on fire. Because want has transformed into need and need into something desperate and all-consuming. "I want this. I want you."

"*Fuck.*" The curse is reverent, almost pained. Then his mouth is on mine again, and coherent thought becomes impossible.

His hand *finally* slides under my sports bra, cupping my breast, thumb brushing across the sensitive peak. The sensation shoots straight through me, and the sound that escapes is definitely not appropriate for a gym.

"So responsive," he murmurs against my mouth. "So perfect. Do you have any idea how many times I've imagined this? How many cold showers have I taken thinking about touching you like this?"

"Show me." The demand comes out breathy, desperate. "Stop imagining and show me."

Something shifts in him, something darker, more primal. His hand slides from my breast to my throat, not squeezing, just resting there in a gesture of possession that should probably alarm me, but instead sends heat flooding through my body.

"You want me to show you?" His voice drops lower, dangerous. "You want to see what the monster wants to do to you?"

"Yes." No hesitation. No fear. Just burning curiosity, trust, and want that's been building for days.

His thumb presses gently against my pulse point, feeling it race. "When I take you, and I will take you, *tesoro,* it won't be gentle. It won't be sweet. I've spent too long holding back, and when I finally let go…" He leans in, his mouth brushing my ear. "I'm going to make you mine in every way that matters. Mark your skin. Make you scream my name. Fuck you until the only word you remember is 'more.' "

Oh God. Every word sends liquid heat through my veins. His hand on my throat, his thigh between my legs, his voice painting pictures of exactly what he wants to do. It's overwhelming, perfect, and not nearly enough.

"I want that." I can barely form words. "I want all of it."

"No, you don't. Not yet." He pulls back just enough to look at me, and what's in his eyes makes my breath catch—desire, darkness, and something almost like fear. "You think you know what you're signing up for, but you don't. You don't know how possessive I get. How controlling. How dark my needs run when it comes to taking what's *mine*."

"Then tell me. Show me. Stop protecting me from yourself."

His hand tightens fractionally on my throat, not enough to restrict, just enough to send an unequivocal message about who's in control. "In the bedroom, I demand complete submission. Complete trust. When I tell you to do something, you do it. No questions, no hesitation."

"Okay."

"It's not okay. Because if you give me that control, I'll take everything... your pleasure, your pain, your surrender. I'll push boundaries you didn't know you had." His thumb strokes the side of my neck, a gentle contrast to his words. "And when I'm done, you'll be marked, claimed, completely mine in ways that terrify you and thrill you in equal measure."

The clinical, detached Alessandro from training has completely disappeared. In his place is the man Marco warned me about—dangerous, possessive, dark. The real Alessandro De Luca, The Shadow, is showing me exactly what lives beneath the surface.

And heaven help me, it's the hottest thing I've ever experienced.

"I trust you." The words come out steadier than expected. "I trust you not to hurt me. Not to take more than I can give."

"That's the problem." His forehead drops to mine, breathing hard. "I don't trust myself not to. Not with you. Not when wanting you has become the only thing that feels real in my world of blood and violence."

"Alessandro."

"No." He steps back abruptly, and the loss of his heat, touch, and presence is almost painful. "Not like this. Not in a gym where anyone could walk in. Not when I'm barely holding onto control."

"I don't *want* you to hold onto control. I want you to *let go*."

"You say that now." He rakes a hand through his hair, and he looks wrecked, lips swollen from kissing, eyes dark with want, breathing ragged. "But when you see what letting go actually looks like..."

"Then I'll decide if I can handle it. Stop making decisions for me!" Frustration bleeds into the words. "Stop assuming you know what I can or can't take. I'm a grown woman who knows her own mind."

"You're a woman who's been shot at, threatened, and forced to hide in a penthouse because of me.

Forgive me for wanting to protect you from one more dark thing."

"You're not protecting me, you're protecting yourself." The accusation rings out in the gym. "You're scared that if you show me who you really are, I'll run. But Alessandro, I've seen you threaten people, carry guns, and orchestrate violence. I know who you are. And I'm still here."

"You know the surface. You don't know what I'm like when all the restraints come off."

"Then show me." Closing the distance puts us face-to-face again. "Tonight. Your room. No holding back, no protecting me from yourself. Just you, me, and the truth of what this is."

His jaw works as an internal battle plays out across his features. "You don't know what you're asking."

"I'm asking for honesty. For you to stop treating our relationship like it's another security problem to be managed." My hands frame his face, forcing eye contact. "I want all of you, Alessandro. The good, the bad, the dark. Stop making me beg for what should be freely given."

"Elena—"

"Do you want me?" The question is simple, direct.

"More than breathing."

"Do you trust me?"

"With everything."

"Then take a leap of faith. Let me in. Really in."
Rising on tiptoes brings our mouths close to
touching. "I promise I'm stronger than you think."

He's silent for a long moment, dark eyes
searching mine. "Tonight. But Elena, when this
happens, when I finally stop holding back, there's
no going back. You'll be mine in every way that
matters. Body, heart, soul. All of it."

"Good. Because you're already *mine*."

The possessive satisfaction that crosses his face
should probably concern me. Instead, it sends
anticipation curling through my stomach.

"Tonight," he repeats. "But first, I have business
to handle."

"Business. Right. The mysterious, dangerous
business you won't tell me about."

"It's better if you don't know the details."

"*Alessandro.*"

"Please." The word stops me cold because he
never says please. Never asks instead of demands.
"Please let me handle this my way. Let me keep
some of the darkness away from you for a little
while longer."

With the raw honesty in his voice, the
vulnerability lurking beneath the command, it's
impossible to argue with.

"Fine. But you come back to me. Safe. In one
piece. Or I'm coming after you myself."

A smile tugs at his mouth, the first real smile in

days. "Are you trying to scare me?"

"I'm telling you how I want this to end. You here with me."

"I'll hold you to it." He kisses me. It's soft, sweet, and nothing like the consuming heat from moments ago. "Tonight, *tesoro*. Be ready."

"For what?"

His smile turns wicked. "For everything."

Then he's gone, leaving me alone in the gym with a racing pulse, trembling legs, and the absolute certainty that tonight is going to change everything.

The rest of the day drags. I have lunch with Alessandro's chef, trying to make conversation while questions spin through my head. What constitutes '*everything?*' How dark is dark? What exactly does submission look like with a man like Alessandro?

More importantly, why do all those questions make heat pool low in my belly instead of fear?

Mira calls around three, her voice concerned. "Lena, where are you? The shop's been closed for days, and you're not answering texts."

"I'm sorry. Something came up. Family emergency." The lie tastes bitter, but what's the alternative? *'Hey, Mira, I'm actually hiding from the mafia in my mob boss boyfriend's penthouse because someone threw a brick through my window?'*

"Oh no! Is everything okay? Do you need anything?"

"Everything's fine. I'll be back soon." Another lie. Because nothing about this situation is fine, and 'soon' depends entirely on when Alessandro neutralizes whatever threat Greco poses.

"Okay, but seriously, call if you need anything. And when you're back, we're getting drinks, and you're telling me everything."

"Deal."

The call ends, and guilt sits heavy in my chest—lying to my best friend, hiding in a fortress, waiting for a man to come back from doing God knows what so we can finally cross the line we've been dancing around for days.

This isn't the life I imagined when opening a flower shop and the future Nonna would have wanted, full of danger, secrets, and loving a man who kills people.

But thinking about Alessandro, about the way he looks at me like I'm precious, the way he touches me as if I might break, the way he's trying so hard to protect me even from himself, walking away isn't possible.

Maybe that makes me crazy or stupid. Or maybe, just maybe, it makes me exactly the kind of woman who can love a man like Alessandro De Luca.

Seven o'clock comes and goes.

No Alessandro.

Eight o'clock.

Still nothing.

By nine, pacing has worn a path in the living room floor. The security team refuses to answer questions about his location. The phone goes to voicemail.

What if something happened? What if Greco made a move, and Alessandro is hurt or worse, and nobody's telling me because they think protecting me means keeping me in the dark?

At 9:47 p.m., the elevator finally dings.

Alessandro steps out, and relief floods through me so powerfully it's almost painful. He's alive. He's here. He's—

Covered in blood.

Not his blood, at least. It doesn't look like his blood. But there's spatter on his shirt, his hands, even a few drops on his face. He looks like he walked out of a horror movie, and the cold emptiness in his eyes is more terrifying than the blood.

"Alessandro." His name comes out as a whisper. "What happened?"

He looks at me as though he's seeing me from a great distance. "You should go to your room."

"What? *No*. What happened? Are you hurt?"

"I'm fine. But you should go to your room." His voice is flat, emotionless. The voice of The Shadow, not Alessandro. "Please, Elena. Don't see me like this."

But how can looking away be possible when he's

standing there covered in evidence of whatever violence he committed tonight? When the man who promised to show me everything is trying to hide again?

"*No*." The word comes out firm. "You said tonight. You said no more holding back. So don't hide from me now."

His jaw clenches. "This is what I was trying to protect you from. This is what holding back looks like when it stops."

"Then show me. Tell me what happened."

For a long moment, he stares. Then, slowly, he moves toward the kitchen. His jacket gets shrugged off. It's ruined, blood-soaked. The shoulder holster comes next, gun still nestled in leather. His shirt follows, revealing the tattoos covering his torso, Italian script, religious imagery, things that probably mean something in his world.

"Greco's lieutenant made a move on one of our warehouses," he says, voice still flat. "He tried to take out six of my men. He thought he could weaken my operation."

"What did you do?"

"What I always do. I made an example." He turns on the sink to wash his hands. The water runs pink, then red, then pink again. "He won't be making any more moves."

"You killed him."

"Yes."

The simple affirmation should shock me or send me running. Instead, watching him methodically wash blood from his hands, all that exists is concern for the emptiness in his eyes.

"How many others?"

"Three of his men. The rest ran." The water shuts off. He dries his hands on a towel, movements mechanical. "I wanted them to run. Wanted them to spread the word about what happens when you come after what's mine."

"*Alessandro.*"

"This is what I am, Elena." He finally looks at me, and the bleakness in his eyes makes my chest ache. "This is what you're choosing. A man who kills without hesitation. Who uses violence as a tool. Who came home tonight covered in blood and felt nothing except satisfaction that the message was sent."

The words are meant to scare me.

Meant to push me away.

Meant to show me the monster he thinks he is.

But all that's visible is a man trying desperately to protect me from himself. A man who thinks his darkness makes him unworthy of light.

So instead of running, instead of showing fear, disgust, or any of the reactions he's expecting, the distance between us closes. Arms wrap around him despite the blood, despite the violence he represents, despite everything.

"You came back to me," I speak the words against his chest. "That's all that matters."

His entire body goes rigid. "Elena, you shouldn't—"

"I know what I should and shouldn't do. And right now, I should hold you. Because you're shaking, you think you're a monster, and someone needs to remind you, you're human."

"Human." He laughs, bitter and broken. "Human monsters are the worst kind."

"You're not a monster. You're a man doing what he has to do to survive in an impossible world." I pull back just enough to meet his eyes. "Now go shower. Then come to bed. And stop trying to scare me away. It's not working."

He stares at me like solving an impossible equation. Then, slowly, his hands come up to frame my face. "You're going to be the death of me."

"Or your salvation. I haven't decided yet."

The laugh that escapes is more real this time. "Go to my room. Wait for me there. And Elena?"

"Yes?"

"Thank you. For not running."

"I told you, I'm *not* going anywhere."

His kiss is soft, reverent, tasting of gratitude, wonder, and something that might be hope.

Then he's gone to shower away the blood, leaving me alone to wait in his bedroom.

Tonight, darkness and light are finally going to

stop fighting. Tonight, Alessandro De Luca is going to learn that some people are strong enough to love monsters. And maybe that's exactly what turns monsters back into men.

10

Alessandro

The shower runs hot enough to scald, washing away blood and violence, but not the memory of Elena's arms around me. Not the way she held me despite everything—the blood, the admission, the darkness that should have sent her running.

Steam fills the bathroom as hands brace against the marble tile. Three men are dead tonight. Greco's lieutenant is bleeding out on a warehouse floor. The message sent in the only language the underworld understands.

And Elena waited. Didn't run. Told me to come to bed.

The water shuts off. A towel wraps around my hips. In the mirror, the reflection shows exactly what years of this life have created—scars crossing my torso from knife fights and bullets, tattoos covering most of the damage, dark circles under eyes that have seen too much.

Not the kind of man who deserves what's waiting in the bedroom.

But for once, selfishness wins over self-preservation.

When I enter the bedroom, every coherent thought evaporates.

Elena is lying on the bed, my bed, wearing nothing but one of my white dress shirts and black lace panties that should be illegal. The shirt is unbuttoned just enough to show the curve of her breasts, sleeves rolled up to her elbows. Her dark hair spreads across my pillow like silk, and those honey-colored eyes are watching me with a heat that goes straight through my chest.

"Hi," she says softly, like she's not currently destroying every defense mechanism built over fifteen years.

"Hi." The word comes out rougher than intended. "You're in my bed."

"I am. You told me to wait here." She sits up slowly, the movement making the shirt gape open further. "Having second thoughts?"

Second, third, and fourth thoughts. Because walking across this room means crossing a line that can't be uncrossed. Means taking this beautiful, innocent woman and marking her as *mine* in ways she can't fully comprehend yet.

But her eyes hold no fear. No hesitation. Just want, trust, and stubborn determination.

"Last chance to run, *tesoro*." The warning comes out dark, promising. "After this, you're *mine*. Completely. No going back."

"Stop trying to scare me." She rises to her knees on the bed, and the sight of her like that, in my shirt, on my sheets, looking at me like I'm something other than a monster, nearly breaks my control. "I want this. I want you. Stop making me wait."

The distance between the door and the bed closes in three strides. Her sharp inhale when my hand tangles in her hair, tilting her head back, is the most satisfying sound in the world.

"When I take you, it won't be gentle." The words are delivered against her throat, feeling her pulse race beneath my lips. "I'm going to use you, take everything you're offering, and then demand more. I'm going to make you scream, make you beg, make you forget every man who came before me."

"Yes." The word comes out breathy. "God, yes."

"Safe word. Choose one now."

Her eyes meet mine, pupils blown wide with desire. "Red."

"Good girl." The praise makes her shiver. "Now tell me, have you ever let a man completely control your pleasure?"

"No."

"Have you ever been truly dominated? Pushed

past what you thought were your limits?"

"No." Her breath hitches as my free hand slides under the shirt, splaying across her stomach. "Alessandro."

"Have you ever been fucked by a man who knows exactly what he wants and takes it without apology?"

"No." The admission is almost a whimper.

"Then you're in for an education." The shirt gets stripped off in one smooth motion, leaving her in nothing but those black lace panties. "Cristo, look at you."

She's perfect.

Absolutely perfect.

Skin like cream, curves in all the right places, nipples already hard and begging for attention. The urge to worship every inch of her wars with the need to take, possess, and claim.

Taking wins.

"On your knees. At the edge of the bed. *Now*."

She moves without hesitation, repositioning herself exactly where instructed. The obedience sends satisfaction coursing through me.

"Good. Now, this is how tonight works. You do exactly what I tell you, when I tell you, how I tell you. No questioning, no hesitating. Your job is to take what I give you and ask for more." My hand traces the line of her spine, feeling her tremble. "Think you can handle that?"

"Yes."

"Yes, what?"

She catches on immediately. "Yes, Alessandro."

"Better." The towel drops, and her eyes widen at the sight of exactly how much I want her. "But I think we can do better than that. When we're like this, when I'm giving orders, and you're obeying, you call me 'sir.' Understand?"

"Yes, sir."

The words go straight to my cock. "Open that pretty mouth, *tesoro.* Show me what you can do."

She leans forward without hesitation, and when her lips wrap around me, warm, wet, and perfect, a groan tears from my throat. She starts slow, tentative, clearly trying to figure out what I like.

"Deeper." The command comes out harshly. "Take more. I want to feel the back of your throat."

She tries, eyes watering slightly as she pushes past her limit. Her hand comes up to grip what won't fit, and the sight of her on her knees, mouth stretched around me, trying so hard to please, it's almost enough to end this before it begins.

"That's it. Good girl." Fingers tangle in her hair, not controlling yet, just holding. "Now relax your throat. Let me in."

She does, and the sensation when she finally takes me deep enough to choke makes my vision blur. The instinct to hold her there, to use her mouth until I come down her throat, is overwhelming.

But no. Not yet. Tonight is about showing her exactly what belonging to me means, and that means her pleasure comes first.

Even if making her wait is part of the torture.

"Enough." Pulling back takes more willpower than facing down Greco's men. "On your back. Middle of the bed. Spread your legs."

She scrambles to obey, sprawling across dark sheets like an offering. The black lace panties are soaked through. She's been this turned on the whole time.

"Please," she whispers.

"Please, what? Use your words."

"Please touch me. Please, I need..."

"You need what?" The mattress dips as I move over her, caging her body with mine. "Tell me exactly what you need, Elena."

"I need you. Inside me. Making me yours." Her hips tilt, seeking friction. "Please, sir."

The 'sir' nearly breaks my control. "Soon. But first..." My mouth finds her breast, teeth grazing the sensitive peak. "First, I'm going to make you come so hard you forget your name."

My hand slides down her stomach, over the lace, feeling how wet she is. "Cristo, you're soaked. All this from sucking my cock?"

"Yes. God, yes." Her back arches when my fingers find her clit through the lace. "Please."

"Patience." The panties are ripped off, tossed aside, leaving her completely bare beneath me. "Beautiful. So fucking beautiful."

My mouth follows the path my hands blazed, down her neck, across her breasts, over her stomach. Her thighs fall open automatically, and the trust in that gesture makes something in my chest crack.

"Alessandro..." His name becomes a moan when my mouth finds her center. "Oh God."

"No god here, *tesoro.* Just me. Just this." My tongue circles her clit, tasting her arousal. "Just you falling apart because I'm making you."

She tastes like heaven, sin, and everything I don't deserve. My fingers join my mouth, sliding inside her heat, and she's so tight, so perfect, clenching around the intrusion.

"More," she gasps. "Please, more."

"Greedy." But I add another finger, curling them to hit that spot inside that makes her cry out. "That's it. Take what I give you."

My mouth works her clit while my fingers fuck her mercilessly, and within minutes, she's trembling, on the edge, desperate. But I don't let her fall. Every time she gets close, I back off, keeping her suspended in that perfect torture.

"Please." She's begging now, exactly like I wanted. "Please, I need... I can't—"

"You can. You will. You'll come when I tell you to

come and not before." My free hand slides up to grip her throat, not choking, just holding, reminding her who's in control. "Now, be a good girl and give me what's *mine*."

My fingers curl hard inside her, my thumb replacing my mouth on her clit, and the combination finally pushes her over. She comes with a scream that echoes off the walls, her body bowing off the bed, clenching so hard around my fingers it's almost painful.

Beautiful. Absolutely beautiful.

She's still shaking when I slide up her body, positioning myself at her entrance. "Look at me. I want to see your eyes when I take you."

Her gaze meets mine, dazed, satisfied, but still hungry. "Please."

"Please, what?"

"Please fuck me, sir."

Those three words destroy the last shred of my restraint. I push inside in one hard thrust, and the sensation of her heat, tightness, and body stretching to accommodate me, Cristo, nothing has ever felt this good.

"Alessandro!" My name tears from her throat.

"*Mine*." The word comes out possessive, claiming. "Say it. Tell me you're *mine*."

"*Yours*. God, I'm yours."

"Good girl." My hips move, setting a brutal pace that has her gasping with every thrust. "This is what you wanted. What you begged for. My cock inside you, fucking you like you're *mine* to use."

"Yes, please, don't stop."

No intention of stopping. Not when she feels this perfect. Not when every sound she makes drives me closer to the edge. Not when her nails are digging into my back hard enough to leave marks that will serve as reminders tomorrow.

"Touch yourself." Again, the command comes out harshly. "I want to feel you come on my cock."

Her hand slides between our bodies, finding her clit, and the added sensation makes her clench harder around me. "I'm close, so close..."

"Not yet. Hold it." My hand finds her throat again, applying just enough pressure to make her gasp. "You come when I tell you. Understand?"

"Yes, sir." The words are broken, desperate. "Please, I can't hold it much longer..."

"Roll over. On your hands and knees."

I pull out, ignoring her whimper at the loss, and manhandle her into position. This angle lets me go deeper, lets me see the curve of her spine, the way her ass looks raised for me.

"Beautiful." One hand grips her hip hard enough to bruise. The other tangles in her hair, pulling her head back. "You're going to take everything I give you. Every. Single. Inch."

The thrust back inside makes her cry out, and this position somehow feels even better. Deeper.

More possessive. Like I'm claiming territory that will always belong to me.

"Next time..." my voice comes out dark with promise, "... I'm going to take this ass too. Going to fill every hole, mark you everywhere, make sure there's not an inch of you that doesn't remember who you belong to."

"Yes." She's barely coherent now, lost in sensation. "Anything, everything, just don't stop!"

My hand releases her hair and slides around to find her clit again, circling the sensitive bundle with practiced precision. "Come. *Now*. Come for me, Elena."

She shatters, screaming my name, her body clenching so hard around me that it triggers my release. I empty inside her with a groan that sounds almost pained, hips jerking through aftershocks as she milks every drop.

For a long moment, neither of us moves. Then, carefully, I pull out and gather her against my chest, both of us breathing hard and trembling.

"You okay?" The question comes out rough with concern.

"Okay doesn't begin to cover it." Her laugh is shaky but genuine. "That was... God, Alessandro, that was..."

"Too much?"

"Perfect." She turns in my arms to face me, and the satisfaction in her expression eases something in my chest. "That was absolutely perfect."

"Good." I kiss her forehead, gentle in contrast to everything that just happened. "Because we're not done yet."

Her eyes widen. "Not done?"

"Not even close. You said you wanted everything, *tesoro*. I'm going to spend all night showing you exactly what that means."

The next few hours blur together, her mouth on me again, me buried inside her against the window with the city spread below us, her riding me while I watched her take her pleasure. By the time exhaustion finally wins, the sheets are destroyed, and Elena is marked with my fingerprints on her hips, teeth marks on her shoulders, evidence everywhere that she belongs to me.

She falls asleep tucked against my side, sated, trusting, and completely unaware that giving her body to me has sealed her fate in ways she can't comprehend yet.

Mine. In every way that matters. No going back.

The thought should satisfy the possessive thing living in my chest. And it does for about three hours.

Then my phone rings.

Marco's voice comes through tense, urgent. "Boss, we have a problem."

"What kind of problem?" Keeping my voice low to avoid waking Elena takes effort.

"Greco. He's talking to the Feds."

Every muscle goes rigid. "Since when?"

"Apparently months. We just got confirmation from our source in the Bureau. He's building a case, not only against us, but against every major family in the city."

"*Fuck.*" The word is whispered but vicious. "How much does he have?"

"Enough to be a problem. Names, transactions, locations. If he flips officially, we're looking at federal indictments across the board."

Which means RICO charges. Which means life in prison. Which means Elena would be caught in the crossfire of a federal investigation.

"Pull everyone back. Clean up anything that could connect to federal charges. And Marco? Find out who else knows about this. If Greco's talking to the Feds, someone had to facilitate the introduction."

"On it. Boss, the girl needs to know. If the Feds are investigating, they'll find out about her. She'll be questioned, maybe charged as an accessory."

"She's not an accessory. She knows nothing."

"Doesn't matter. They'll use her to pressure you. You know how this works."

Yes. Unfortunately, knowing exactly how this works is the problem. Elena would become a target, not only from Greco but from federal prosecutors looking to flip witnesses, from rival families who'd use her as leverage, from every direction.

"I'll handle it."

"How?"

Good question. "I'll figure something out. Just keep me posted on the Fed situation."

The call ends, and Elena stirs beside me, making a sleepy sound. "Everything okay?"

"Fine. Just business. Go back to sleep."

She settles again, trusting, and guilt sits heavily in my chest. Tonight was supposed to be about honesty. About showing her everything. About no more secrets.

But how can the truth be told when the truth is that loving me might destroy her life in ways she can't imagine, when federal investigations, RICO charges, and witness protection programs might become her new reality?

Sleep refuses to return. Instead, the hours pass watching Elena sleep, memorizing the way she looks in my bed, the way she fits against me, the way she chose me despite every reason not to.

And planning. Always planning. How to protect her. How to keep her away from the fallout that's coming. How to make sure that when this all falls apart, and it *will* fall apart, eventually, she walks away clean.

Even if that means pushing her away first.

Morning comes too soon. Elena wakes slowly, stretching like a cat, then wincing slightly. "I'm going to feel this for days."

"Good." The satisfaction in the word is real. "I want you remembering exactly who you belong to."

She laughs, then notices my expression. "What's wrong?"

"Nothing. I just..." The sentence dies because how do you tell someone you just claimed in every possible way you might have to let them go to keep them safe?

"Alessandro." She sits up, concern replacing satisfaction. "Talk to me. What happened?"

"Business complications. Nothing you need to worry about."

"Don't do that. Don't shut me out now. Not after..." She gestures at the destroyed bed, the evidence of what we shared. "Not after that."

She deserves the truth, honesty, and better than a man who's dragging her into federal investigations, turf wars, and violence.

"There's..." The words stick. "There might be some legal complications coming. Federal attention. It's probably nothing, but—"

"But it could be something." She's already reading between the lines, already seeing the implications. "What kind of federal attention?"

"The kind that asks uncomfortable questions about who you associate with. The kind that might try to use you as leverage against me."

Her face goes pale. "They would come after me?

Even though I haven't done anything?"

"Association is enough in federal cases. And, *tesoro*, you're very clearly associated with me now." Gesturing at the marks on her skin makes the point without words.

She processes this, and watching her realize exactly what being *mine* actually costs is harder than any bullet taken.

"Okay." Her voice is steady, but fear lurks in her eyes. "Okay. What do we do?"

"We? There's no *we* in this decision. You need to—"

The bedroom door crashes open.

Marco stands in the doorway, face grim, holding a tablet. "Boss, you need to see this. *Now*."

"I'm busy—"

"*Now*." Marco's tone brooks no argument. "It's about her."

Elena pulls the sheet up, suddenly aware of her nudity, but Marco doesn't even glance her way. His attention is fixed on me, and whatever is on that tablet has him rattled enough to violate my privacy.

"Show me."

He crosses to the bed and turns the tablet around. On the screen is a news article in the *Seattle Times* posted two hours ago.

The headline makes my blood run cold.

A Merry Little Vendetta

Federal Investigation Targets
Seattle Crime Families:
Dozens Expected to Face Charges.

But it's the photograph beneath the headline that stops my heart. Elena, leaving her flower shop. The caption reads...

Elena Harper, Owner of Petals & Pines,
Reportedly Linked to
Alessandro 'The Shadow' De Luca,
Suspected Head of the De Luca Crime Family

"How..." Elena's voice is small, shocked. "How do they know? How did the—"

"Russo," Marco says the name like a curse. "Your grandparents' last name was Russo. Same as the family we're at war with. The Feds think you're connected, either a plant, or collateral, or leverage. Either way, you're now part of their investigation."

"But I'm not, I don't have anything to do with..." She's looking at me now, fear and confusion warring in her expression. "Alessandro, tell them. Tell them I'm not involved."

"It doesn't matter what I tell them." The words come out flat. "They'll investigate you anyway. Question you. Tear apart your life looking for connections. And Elena, they'll find them. They'll find the texts, the calls, the fact that you've been living in my penthouse. They'll twist everything into proof of involvement."

"No." She's shaking her head. "No, this isn't happening. I run a flower shop. I'm not a criminal. I haven't done anything wrong."

"You fell in love with me." The admission is bitter. "It's enough to destroy your life."

She stares at me, and I watch the realization hit, watch her understand exactly what being with me actually costs, is worse than any physical pain.

"Get out." Her voice is quiet, deadly.

"Elena—"

"*Get. Out.*" Louder now, trembling with fury. "Both of you. Out of this room. Out of my sight. Out of my life."

"You don't mean that—"

"Don't I?" She's out of bed, grabbing my shirt from the floor and pulling it on with shaking hands. "You knew. You knew this could happen, and you still..." Her voice breaks. "You still took everything from me. My safety, my reputation, my future. You took it all and didn't even warn me."

"I was trying to protect you."

"By fucking me?" The accusation cuts. "By marking me, claiming me, making sure everyone knows I belong to you? That's protection?"

"It's complicated."

"It's *selfish*!" She's shouting now, tears streaming down her face. "You wanted me, so you took me, and you didn't care what it would cost me. You didn't care that my name is now in the paper, linked to organized crime. My shop will suffer. My life is ruined because I was stupid enough to fall for your damn lies."

"They weren't lies."

"*Get. Out!*" She grabs the nearest thing, a lamp, and throws it. The crash against the wall echoes like a gunshot. "Get out before I call the police myself and tell them everything."

Marco grabs my arm. "Boss, we need to go."

But leaving Elena like this, furious, terrified, and feeling betrayed, every instinct screams against it.

"Elena, please."

"I said, *get out!*" Another throw, a book this time. "And don't come back. Don't call, don't text, don't send your men to watch my shop. We're done. You hear me? *Done!*"

Marco physically pulls me from the room before more projectiles can be launched. The door slams behind us, and the sound of Elena's sobbing carries through the walls.

"Boss."

"*Don't.*" The word comes out broken. "Just don't."

Three hours ago, she was in my arms, sated, trusting, and mine. Now she's behind that door, crying because being with me has destroyed her life.

Marco was right. The men were right. Caring

about her made me sloppy, made me selfish, made me put what I wanted over what she needed.

And now she's paying the price.

"What do you want to do?" Marco asks quietly.

"Damage control. Get our lawyers on this. Make sure her name is cleared in any investigation. And Marco? I want round-the-clock protection on her, whether she likes it or not."

"She's going to hate it."

"She already hates me. At least this way she'll be alive to hate me. Take her home. She needs to feel safe and in control."

Back in my office, the tablet shows the article again. Elena's photograph, her shop, her name, all of it connected to mine. All of it evidence of my selfishness, weakness, and failure to protect what matters most.

The phone buzzes.

Unknown Number: *Flowers for you, delivered to the lobby.*

Flowers. From Elena.

The security footage shows her leaving the building two hours ago, face set, eyes red, determination in every line of her body. Shows her entering the lobby thirty minutes ago with a small bouquet. Shows her leaving it with the front desk and walking out without looking back.

The bouquet arrives in my office courtesy of building security. It's elegant, professional, and devastating in its simplicity, black roses, three of them, tied with a white ribbon.

The card reads...

For the death of whatever this was.
Don't contact me again.
~E

Black roses.

Mourning.

Ending.

Death.

She really does know her flowers.

Marco looks at the bouquet, then at me. "Boss..."

"Leave me."

"But—"

"I said, *leave me!*" The roar echoes through the office, and Marco retreats without another word.

Alone with black roses and the wreckage of the best thing to happen in fifteen years, the only option is to stare at Elena's message and accept the truth.

She's right to hate me.

Right to end this.

Right to protect herself from the disaster that loving me creates.

But that doesn't mean I'm letting her go without a fight. Doesn't mean I'm allowing Greco, the Feds, or anyone else to hurt her.

Even if she never speaks to me again, even if she sends a thousand black roses, even if she hates me until the day she dies, she'll be protected.

Because Elena Harper might not be mine anymore.

But she'll always be under *my protection*.

Whether she wants it or not.

Chapter II

Elena

The apartment above Petals & Pines feels emptier than it should.

It's been three days since I walked out of Alessandro's penthouse. Three days since discovering my name in the *Seattle Times* was linked to organized crime. Three days since realizing the man who claimed to love me had destroyed my life without even blinking or warning.

The shop has been slow, customers suddenly remembering they have other florists, other options, anywhere that isn't associated with 'The Shadow.' My phone has blown up with messages from concerned friends, nosy reporters, and one very persistent FBI agent who wants to 'just chat.'

I haven't answered any of them.

The black roses sitting on my counter mock me with their thorny perfection. I sent them to Alessandro three days ago as a final message.

Done.

Finished.

Over.

So why does every part of me ache, as if something vital has been ripped away?

"Stupid," the word is muttered while arranging a bouquet for one of the few remaining loyal customers. "Stupid to fall for him. Stupid to think it could work. *Stupid, stupid, stupid.*"

The shop bell chimes.

"We're closing early today," the announcement comes without looking up. "Sorry, but—"

"Elena Harper?"

The voice is unfamiliar, male, with an accent that's definitely not local. Looking up reveals three men in the shop, all wearing dark jackets and expressions that make every instinct scream danger.

"Can I help you?" The pruning shears are gripped tighter, though what good would they do against three grown men is questionable.

"You can come with us quietly." The speaker is tall, scarred, with dead eyes that have seen too much violence. "Our boss wants to have a conversation."

"Your boss can make an appointment like

everyone else." Keeping my voice steady takes effort. "Now, *get out* of my shop."

"See, that's the thing." He takes a step forward, and the other two fan out. "It's not really a request."

The back room is maybe ten feet away. The panic button Alessandro insisted on installing, the one I swore would never be used, is back there, hidden under the worktable.

"I'm not going anywhere with you." Another step back, trying to calculate distance, angles, and chances. "Leave now, or I'm calling the police."

"The police?" The man laughs. "Sweetheart, the police aren't going to help you. Not when you're De Luca's whore."

The word hits like a slap. "*Get out.*"

"Make us."

They move fast, faster than I expected. One grabs for my arm. The pruning shears swing wildly, catching him across the face. He screams, blood spraying, and for a second, there's hope.

Then the second man has me, arm around my throat, lifting me off my feet. The shears clatter to the floor.

I can't breathe.

I can't think.

I can't—

The front window explodes.

Not from inside. From outside. Someone shooting.

Alessandro's men. The ones he said would watch the shop. Two of them burst through the shattered glass, guns drawn, shouting commands.

The world becomes violent.

Gunfire is so loud and deafening in the enclosed space. The man holding me uses my body as a shield. Hot blood sprays across my face, not mine, someone else's. One of Alessandro's men goes down, the back of his head—

God. Oh God. There's brain matter on the wall. Gray and red and—

Vomit rises but gets swallowed down. I can't be sick. I can't freeze. I have to *move.*

Another of Alessandro's men falls, chest blooming red. He's still alive, gasping, trying to reach his weapon. The scarred man walks over calmly and shoots him point-blank in the face.

The sound is wet, final, horrible, and will haunt my dreams forever.

"Get her in the van!" The scarred man is already moving, and the one holding me drags me backward toward the door. "*Now!*"

Outside, a white van waits with doors open. I'm struggling, fighting, trying to scream, but his arm is crushing the air from my throat. Black spots dance across my vision.

"Stop fighting, bitch." His breath is hot against my ear. "Save your energy. You're going to need it for what comes next."

He throws me into the van. I hit the metal floor hard, pain exploding through my shoulder and hip. Before recovery is possible, they're climbing in, all three of them, pulling the doors shut, the van already moving.

"*Drive!*" The scarred man shouts toward the front. "De Luca's men will be swarming this area in minutes."

Hands grab me, yanking me up, slamming me against the van wall. Zip ties bite into my wrists, securing them behind my back. Another tie is around my ankles.

They're efficient, practiced.

This isn't their first kidnapping.

"Please." The word comes out hoarse, terrified. "Please, I don't know anything. I can't help you."

"We don't need your help." The scarred man crouches in front of me, and his smile is all teeth and malice. "We just need De Luca to know we have you. Need him to understand what happens when you disrespect the Russo family."

Russo family. The rival organization. Greco's people.

"He won't care." The lie comes desperately. "We're not together anymore. I kicked him out. He doesn't—"

"Doesn't what? Care about you?" The man laughs. "Sweetheart, he's had guards on your shop twenty-four seven since you left. Has your

187

apartment bugged. Tracks your every move. The man's obsessed." His hand reaches out, grabbing my face roughly. "Which means you're valuable. Means we can use you."

"Use me how?" But the answer is already visible in their eyes, in the way they're looking at me, in the hunger mixing with violence.

"Well..." The second man, who is younger, with a spider tattoo on his neck, grins. "Boss said not to kill you. Didn't say nothing about having some fun first."

Terror, pure and primal, floods every nerve. "No. No, *please.*"

"What do you think, Bruno?" Spider tattoo looks at the scarred man. "De Luca's girl. Bet she's a good fuck if he's this obsessed."

"I think..." The scarred man's smile widens. "I think De Luca needs to learn a lesson about respect. And what better way than sending him back his girl all used up?"

"*Please.*" Tears are streaming now, and I can't stop them. "Please don't, I'll do anything."

"You're going to do anything anyway." His hand slides down, gripping my throat. "Question is whether you fight and make it worse, or submit and maybe we'll be gentle."

They won't be gentle.

I see it in their eyes, in the way they're already reaching for their belts, in the anticipation making them careless—

The van swerves violently.

Everyone stumbles, thrown off balance. Gunfire erupts from somewhere outside, the distinctive crack of assault rifles.

"*What the fuck*!" The scarred man scrambles toward the front. "What's happening?"

"It's De Luca!" The driver's voice is panicked. "He found us, he's, oh Christ—"

The driver's window explodes. Blood sprays forward. The van careens wildly, tires screaming, and then it impacts hard, slamming everyone against the walls.

Everything stops.

For a moment, silence.

Then the back doors are literally ripped open, the metal screaming as they're torn from hinges, and Alessandro stands silhouetted against the winter sunlight.

But this isn't the Alessandro from the penthouse, or the flower shop, or even the man covered in blood three nights ago.

This is The Shadow.

His face is absolutely blank, no rage, no fear, nothing human in his expression. In one hand is a gun. In the other, a knife that gleams with fresh blood.

"*Mine*." The word comes out soft, deadly. "She's *mine*."

He moves like death itself.

The third man, the one who hadn't spoken, reaches for his weapon. Alessandro's gun barks once. The man's head snaps back, eyes going vacant, body crumpling.

Spider tattoo lunges with a knife. Alessandro disarms him in two moves by grabbing his wrist and twisting, the wet crack of breaking bone fills the van. The knife transfers to Alessandro's hand and buries itself in the man's throat. Blood sprays, hot and arterial. The spider tattoo gurgles, clutching uselessly at his neck, and Alessandro watches him fall with those dead, emotionless eyes.

The scarred man, Bruno, has his gun out now, pointed at Alessandro. "One more step, and I blow your head off, De Luca."

"You can try." Alessandro doesn't stop moving. "But you'll be dead before the bullet leaves the chamber. Your choice."

"I've got your girl." Bruno shifts, pressing the gun to my temple. Cold metal against skin makes everything sharper. "Drop your weapons, or she dies."

Alessandro's eyes finally focus on me. For just a second, something human flickers there. Fear. Rage. Pain. Then it's gone, replaced by a terrible emptiness.

"You touch her..." Alessandro says conversationally, "... and I will spend the rest of your very short life making you beg for death. I will peel the skin from your bones. I will keep you alive while I feed you your own organs. I will make you watch as I destroy everything and everyone you've ever cared about before I finally let you die."

Bruno's hand trembles slightly. "Big talk for a man whose girl is about to get her brains splattered."

Alessandro's gun rises and fires.

The bullet takes Bruno in the shoulder, the one holding the gun to my head. His arm jerks back, weapon clattering. He screams, stumbling, trying to regain his weapon.

Alessandro is on him.

What happens next will live in nightmares forever.

Alessandro's knife finds Bruno's stomach. Once. Twice. Three times. Each thrust is precise, clinical, and designed to cause maximum pain without quick death. Bruno's screams turn to gurgles as blood fills his lungs.

"You threatened what's *mine*." Alessandro's voice is still conversational despite the violence. "You put your hands on her. You thought about *raping* her."

The knife finds Bruno's groin. The scream that follows isn't human.

"This is what happens." Another stab, this one to the thigh, the femoral artery opening in a spray of red. "This is what I do to men who touch what belongs to *me*."

Bruno collapses, bleeding out fast now, hands scrabbling uselessly at the wounds. Alessandro watches him die with no expression at all.

Then he turns to me.

The transformation is instantaneous. The dead eyes become human again, concerned, terrified, and devastated. The monster becomes a man.

"Elena." His hands are gentle as his knife slices through the zip ties. "Cristo, Elena, I'm sorry. I'm so sorry. Are you hurt? Did they..."

"They didn't." The words come out shaky. "You got here before, they didn't..."

The zip ties fall away. His arms come around me, and the dam breaks. Sobbing against his chest, surrounded by bodies, blood, and the aftermath of violence, but all that exists is his warmth, his presence, the way his hands shake as they hold me.

"I've got you." His voice is wrecked. "You're safe. I've got you. Nobody's going to hurt you. I promise. I promise."

"You came." I can't stop crying. "How did you, they killed your men, how did you—"

"Tracking your phone. I asked Marco to keep an eye on it. You didn't think I'd leave you without being able to track you? Did you?" His laugh is broken. "I've been tracking you since you left. When the signal started moving, when my men didn't respond—"

He doesn't finish.

Doesn't need to.

The bodies around us tell the story clearly enough.

"We need to move."

Marco appears at the van opening. "Police will be here soon. And boss, the Feds. We need to clean this up fast."

"Get a crew here. I want this van to disappear, and these bodies dumped where they'll be found. Send Greco a message he can't ignore." Alessandro is already lifting me, cradling me against his chest like something precious. "And Marco? Pull everyone back from Elena's shop. She was right... the protection makes her a target."

"Boss..."

"She was right. I made her a target by claiming her." His arms tighten around me. "Find another way. Something she won't notice. Something that won't paint a sign on her back."

Marco nods and disappears to coordinate.

Alessandro carries me to a car, not the Mercedes, something nondescript and unremarkable. The driver takes off the moment we're inside, leaving the scene of carnage behind.

"Where are we going?" The question comes out small.

"Safe house. Somewhere nobody knows about." His hand cups my face, thumb brushing away tears. "Elena, I need you to listen to me. What you just saw, what I did—"

"You saved me."

"I butchered three men in front of you."

"You *saved* me." The words come firmer this time. "They were going to, they said they were going to—" I can't finish. Can't say it out loud.

"I know." His jaw clenches. "It's what men like that do, Elena, and I'm so sorry. Cristo, Elena, I've never felt rage like that. Never felt so close to losing control completely."

"But you didn't lose control. You were..." The word comes slowly, surprising even as it's spoken. "Efficient. Precise. You knew exactly what you were doing."

"Yes."

"You've done this before. Killed people like this."

"Yes." No apology. No excuse. Just truth.

I should be terrified, even disgusted, and probably running as far away as possible from a man who stabbed a man repeatedly someone without blinking.

But all that exists is gratitude and relief. The bone-deep certainty Alessandro would burn the entire world down to keep me safe.

"Thank you." The words are whispered against his chest. "For coming. For saving me. Fo-for being what you are."

His entire body goes rigid. "Elena."

"I was wrong." The confession hurts, but needs saying. "Three days ago, when I kicked you out, when I blamed you for everything, I was wrong. Being with you is dangerous. But not being with you is worse. Because those men today? They would have taken me anyway. Would have used me as a message. At least this way, you were there to save me."

"You don't know what you're saying. You're in shock—"

"I know exactly what I'm saying." Pulling back to meet his eyes. "I love you, Alessandro De Luca. I love the man who makes me breakfast and the monster who kills to protect me. I love all of it, all of you, even the parts that terrify me."

"You shouldn't." But his hands are gentle on my face, his eyes searching mine. "You should run far away and never look back."

"Probably. But I'm stubborn, remember? When I want something, I don't give up easily." A shaky smile manages to surface. "And I want you. Even knowing what that costs. Even knowing the danger. I choose *you*."

"Elena..." His voice breaks.

"I choose you," the words are repeated, firmer this time. "Stop trying to push me away for my own good. Stop making decisions for me. Let me love you and love me back, and we'll figure out the rest together."

For a long moment, he simply stares. Then he's kissing me, desperately, tenderly, and tasting of relief, promise, and something that might be hope.

"I love you," he murmurs against my lips. "Cristo, I love you so much it terrifies me."

"Good. Be terrified with me."

His laugh is fractured and broken. "You're going to be the death of me."

"Or your salvation. I haven't decided yet."

The car takes us somewhere safe, a house in the suburbs, nondescript and anonymous. Inside, Alessandro tends to the bruises on my wrists from the zip ties, the scrapes from being thrown in the van, the invisible wounds from almost being—

I can't think about it.

I won't focus on what *almost* happened.

The only thing that matters is that Alessandro found me, saved me, and showed me exactly what loving him truly means.

"Stay with me tonight," the request comes quietly. "Let me hold you and know you're safe."

"I'm not going anywhere," the promise is spoken against his chest as his arms wrap around me. "I'm done running. Done pretending I can live without you. You're stuck with me now."

"Thank God." His hold tightens. "Because letting you walk away three days ago was the hardest thing I've ever done. Watching you hate me, knowing I deserved it..."

"You didn't deserve it. I was scared and angry, and I lashed out." I pull back to meet his eyes. "But Alessandro? No more secrets. No more trying to protect me by hiding things. If we're doing this, *really doing this,* I need all of it. The truth, the danger, everything."

"Everything," he agrees. "No more secrets. No more hiding."

"Good." I press a kiss to his jaw. "Now hold me. And tomorrow, we'll figure out how to handle Greco and the Feds and everyone else who wants to use me against you."

"Tomorrow," he agrees, gathering me close. "Tonight, you're just *mine*, and I'm just *yours*, and nothing else matters."

And surrounded by his warmth, his strength, his love, for the first time in three days, safety finally feels real.

Because monsters might be terrifying.

But sometimes, loving a monster is the only thing that keeps you safe.

And being loved by one is what finally makes them human again.

Chapter 12

Alessandro

Dawn breaks over the safe house, pale winter light filtering through unfamiliar windows. Elena sleeps in my arms, bruised, exhausted, but alive and safe.

The rage from yesterday has cooled into something harder, more purposeful. Greco crossed a line. His men put their hands on what's *mine*, threatened to violate her in ways that still make my blood boil.

They died for it.

But Greco himself remains, and as long as he breathes, Elena is in danger.

Which means the decision was made somewhere around three a.m., watching her sleep, becomes inevitable.

She needs to go. Needs to be somewhere Greco can't reach, somewhere my enemies can't use her as leverage. Somewhere far from the violence that defines my world.

Even if sending her away destroys me.

Her eyes flutter open, focusing on my face. "Morning."

"Morning, *tesoro*." The endearment comes automatically now. "How are you feeling?"

"Sore. Scared." She shifts closer, tucking herself against my chest. "But safe. With you, I feel safe."

The words are a knife to my chest because she shouldn't feel safe. Elena should feel terrified of the man who butchered three people in front of her, who lives in a world where kidnapping and rape threats are Tuesday-afternoon problems.

"Elena, we need to talk."

She stiffens. "Those are never good words."

"No, they're not." Sitting up requires a careful extraction from her warmth. "What happened yesterday, what almost happened, it can't happen again."

"Okay. So, we'll be more careful. More security, better protocols—"

"*No.*" The word comes out harder and colder. "Elena, this isn't about security protocols. This is about the fact that being near me will always put you in danger. Always make you a target. I can't..." The sentence catches. "I can't keep watching you pay the price for *my* choices."

Her expression shifts from confused to

understanding to furious in the span of three seconds. "Don't."

"Don't what?"

"*Don't you dare.*" She's out of bed now, wrapped in one of my shirts, eyes blazing. "Don't you dare use what happened as an excuse to push me away again. We had this conversation. I chose you. *I* choose *you.*"

"You chose before you were almost raped and killed—"

"And I'm still *choosing!*" Her voice rises. "Alessandro, do you think I don't know the risks? Do you think I'm naïve enough to believe loving you will ever be safe or easy? I know what I'm signing up for. Stop treating me like an errant child who can't make her own decisions."

"This isn't about your ability to decide. This is about keeping you alive." Standing puts us face- to- face. "Greco won't stop. And even if we eliminate him, there will be others. There are always others. Rivals, enemies, people looking for any weakness they can exploit. And, *tesoro*, you're my biggest weakness."

"Good." She steps closer, becoming more defiant. "Let them know. Let them all know that hurting me means facing The Shadow's wrath. What you did to those men yesterday… make it a message they can't ignore."

"You don't understand what you're asking."

"I understand perfectly. You want to send me away, put me in witness protection, or ship me off to Italy or whatever plan you've concocted in the last six hours." Her hand presses against my chest, right over my heart. "But here's the thing, I'm *not* going. You can't make me. And if you try, I'll just find my way back."

"Elena—"

"*No*. My turn." Her eyes are fierce and determined. "I love you. Not the sanitized version, not the parts you think are acceptable. *All* of you. The man who makes me breakfast and the monster who kills without hesitation to protect me. The Shadow and Alessandro... I love all of it, and I'm not walking away because loving you is hard."

"Hard doesn't begin to cover what this will be."

"Then let it be impossible. Let it be terrifying and dangerous and completely insane." Her other hand comes up to frame my face. "But let it be us. Together. No more trying to protect me by pushing me away. No more making decisions for my own good. Just you and me against whatever comes."

The words should be easy to argue against. They should be simple to dismantle, grounded in logic, reason, and the cold reality of what tomorrow will bring.

But looking at her, fierce, stubborn, and absolutely certain, arguing becomes impossible.

"You're going to drive me insane." The

observation comes out rough.

"Probably. But you'll never be bored."

"Insane is a significant step beyond bored, *tesoro*."

"You love me anyway." It's not a question.

"Cristo, yes. I love you anyway. Despite my better judgment, despite every logical reason not to, despite knowing this will probably end in disaster." My hands find her waist, pulling her close. "I love you enough to burn the entire world down for you."

"Then stop trying to send me away and let me stay." Her arms wrap around my neck. "Let me be your weakness and your strength. I want to stand beside you, not behind you. Let me love you the way you deserve to be loved, completely, recklessly, and without reservation."

"You have no idea what you're signing up for."

"Then show me. Teach me. Make me yours in every way that matters and stop second-guessing whether I can handle it." She rises on her toes, mouth brushing mine. "I'm stronger than you think, Alessandro De Luca. Strong enough to love a monster. Strong enough to survive your world. I'm strong enough to be exactly what you need."

The kiss that follows erases any remaining resistance. She's right, has been right all along. Sending her away won't keep her safe. It will only separate us while enemies circle. Better to keep her close, protect her properly, and make sure everyone knows that touching Elena Harper means death.

When we finally break apart, both breathing hard, the decision solidifies into certainty.

"Okay," the word comes out rough. "Okay. You stay. But Elena, there are conditions."

"Of course there are."

"Security detail. Non-negotiable. Wherever you go, you have protection."

"Agreed."

"Training continues. Self-defense, weapons handling, situational awareness. You need to be able to protect yourself if I'm not there."

"Also agreed."

"And..." This part is harder. "You need to understand that what I do, the decisions I make, they're not always going to be pretty. Sometimes I'll have to do terrible things. Things that will give you nightmares. Can you live with that?"

She's quiet for a moment, considering. "Can you promise me one thing?"

"Depends on the promise."

"Promise me whatever terrible things you do, they're never to innocent people. That you have lines you won't cross, codes you won't violate. Promise me that the monster has rules."

The request is fair—more than fair. "I promise. No innocents. No women or children. No unnecessary cruelty. Just..." *How to explain the necessity of violence in this world?* "Just what needs to be done to protect what's mine and maintain order."

"Then I can live with it." Her hand finds mine, lacing our fingers together. "Because the alternative, living without you, is worse than any nightmare."

"You're sure? No doubts?"

"Alessandro, I watched you stab a man yesterday, and my first thought was gratitude. I think we're past doubts." A smile tugs at her lips. "Besides, someone has to make sure you eat breakfast and change your bandages. Clearly, you can't be trusted to take care of yourself."

The laugh that escapes is surprised and genuine. "You're insane."

"We've established that. But I'm your brand of insane, which is what matters."

"My brand of insane," the words are repeated, testing them. "I like that."

"Good. Now..." She tugs me back toward the bed. "We have a few hours before your men come to check on us. I suggest we make good use of them."

"Is that so?" The predatory satisfaction that rises is immediate. "And what exactly did you have in mind, *tesoro*?"

"Well..." Her hands slide up my chest. "You did promise to show me everything. And I feel like we've barely scratched the surface of what *everything* means to a man like you."

"Elena." Her name comes out as a warning. "You're playing with fire again."

"I told you, I like the burn."

Any remaining control shatters. My hands grip her hips, lift her, and carry her to the bed. She gasps, half surprise, half anticipation, and the sound goes straight through me.

"If we do this now, it's going to be different than the penthouse." The words come out dark, promising. "The fear from yesterday, the rage, the desperate need to reaffirm you're alive and *mine*, it's all going to come out. And, *tesoro*, I won't be gentle."

"Good." Her legs wrap around my waist. "I don't want gentle. I want everything you've been holding back. Every dark desire, every possessive need, every bit of the monster who saved me. Give it all to me."

Cristo. She's going to be the death of me.

But what a way to die.

The shirt she's wearing, *my shirt*, gets stripped off in one motion. Her bruised wrists catch my attention, the marks from the zip ties darkening to purple. Rage flares fresh at the reminder of what those animals did, what they planned to do.

"*Mine*." The word comes out possessive, primal. "These marks, I'm going to cover them with my own. Replace every reminder of them with reminders of me."

"Yes." Her breath hitches as my mouth finds the bruises, kissing, marking, claiming. "Yours. Only yours."

My hands map her body, every curve, every hollow, every place that makes her gasp. This isn't the exploratory claiming of the penthouse, but rather its reaffirmation. Possession. The desperate need to erase every moment of yesterday's terror with pleasure so intense she forgets how to be afraid.

"Tell me your limits," the demand comes between kisses. "Tell me if there's anything off the table."

"No limits." Her hands are already working my belt. "Take what you want. I trust you."

The trust in those words does something to my chest. She trusts me, The Shadow, the monster, the man covered in yesterday's blood, to take her body and use it however I want. To push boundaries, demand submission, and show her exactly what being mine truly means.

"Safe word still *red*?"

"Yes, sir."

Elena's use of 'sir' makes my cock go hard.

"Good. Because you're going to need it before I'm done with you."

She shivers beneath me, anticipation making her

pupils dilate. My hand slides up her thigh, feeling her tremble.

"First rule, you don't come without permission. I don't care how close you get, how much you want to. You hold it until I tell you otherwise. Understand?"

"Yes, sir."

The immediate obedience sends satisfaction coursing through me. "Good girl. Second rule, I want to hear you. Every gasp, every moan, every time you're close to breaking. Don't hide from me."

"Yes, sir."

My mouth finds her neck, teeth grazing the sensitive skin. She arches into me, already seeking more. But this is about control, mine over her, hers in surrendering it.

"Third rule." My hand slides higher, finding her already wet. "You take everything I give you. Every touch, every command, every moment of pleasure or denial. Your body is *mine* to use as I see fit. Say it."

"My body is yours." Her breath comes faster. "To use as you want."

"Perfect."

My fingers slide inside her, and she gasps, loudly and unrestrained. Her hips tilt, seeking more pressure, more friction. But control means making her wait.

"Please." The word escapes before she can stop it.

"Please, what? Use your words, *tesoro*."

"Please, more. I need—"

"You need what I give you. Nothing more." My thumb finds her clit, circling slowly, too slowly, keeping her on edge. "And right now, I'm giving you this. Be grateful."

"Thank you, sir." The words come breathlessly.

Hours dissolve into sensation. My mouth maps every inch of her skin, finding the places that make her cry out. My hands alternate between gentle and demanding, keeping her guessing. Bringing her to the edge repeatedly, then pulling back, watching her frustration build into desperate need.

"Alessandro, *please*..." She's begging now, exactly where I want her. "Please let me, I can't—"

"You can. You will." My fingers curl inside her, hitting that spot that makes her back arch off the bed. "You'll hold it until I'm ready. Until I've had my fill of watching you fall apart."

When permission finally comes, when she's trembling, incoherent, and so desperate she's nearly sobbing, the release is explosive. She screams my name, her body clenching around my fingers, and the satisfaction of reducing her to this is almost as good as my own pleasure.

Almost.

"Again," the command comes dark. "I want you

to come again. And this time, I'll be inside you while you do."

What follows is primal, her legs wrapped around my waist, nails scoring down my back, both of us lost in the rhythm of bodies claiming and surrendering. When she comes the second time, clenching around me, it triggers my release, deep, claiming, and accompanied by her name torn from my throat.

The third time is slower, more deliberate. She's on her stomach, my hand tangled in her hair, both of us learning new boundaries and testing limits.

"I told you..." my voice comes dark against her ear, "... that next time I'd take this ass too. That I'd claim every part of you."

She tenses slightly beneath me, but doesn't pull away. "I've never—"

"I know." My free hand strokes down her spine, soothing. "We'll go slow. But, *tesoro*, when I'm done, there won't be a single part of you that doesn't belong to me. What is your safe word if it's too much."

"Red," she whispers, reminding us both.

"Good girl."

Preparation takes time, oil slicked between her cheeks, fingers working carefully, stretching and preparing while she gasps and trembles beneath me. The first finger makes her tense, but my other hand slides beneath her, finding her clit, giving pleasure to balance the unfamiliar intrusion.

"Breathe," the command comes gently. "Relax into it. Let me in."

She does, her body gradually accepting the invasion. One finger becomes two, her breathing becoming ragged as sensation overwhelms her.

"Alessandro." His name is half prayer, half plea.

"I've got you. Trust me."

When she's finally ready, when her body has adjusted, and she's writhing beneath me, seeking more, positioning comes carefully. The blunt head of my cock presses against that tight ring of muscle, and her entire body goes rigid.

"Easy. Breathe. Push back against me, yes, like that."

The first breach is exquisite torture. She's impossibly tight, her body resisting even as she tries to relax. My hand finds her clit again, circling, providing pleasure to offset the burn of penetration.

"Too much." Her voice breaks. "It's too—"

"Color, Elena. Give me a color."

A pause. Then, "Yellow. Not red, it's intense."

"Yellow means we pause." Immediately stilling, despite every instinct screaming to push forward. "Breathe. Let your body adjust. We have all the time in the world."

Long moments pass, and her breathing evens. The tension in her shoulders gradually releases. My fingers continue their gentle work on her clit, keeping her aroused, keeping pleasure flowing.

"Okay," she finally whispers. "Okay, I'm ready. More."

"You're sure?"

"Yes, sir. Please. I want, I want all of you. Everywhere."

The last of my control fractures. Slowly, so slowly, pressing deeper. Her body yields inch by inch, accepting the invasion, until I'm finally fully seated. The sensation is overwhelming, heat, pressure, and possession so complete it borders on sacred.

"Cristo." The word is torn from my throat. "Elena, you feel—"

"Full." She gasps. "So full, Alessandro."

"I know, *tesoro*. I know." My hand tangles tighter in her hair, the other still working her clit. "You're taking me so perfectly. Taking everything I'm giving you."

Movement starts slow, shallow thrusts that make her gasp and whimper. But as her body adjusts, as pleasure builds to overwhelm the burn, the rhythm increases. Deeper. Harder. My hips are driving forward while my fingers work her clit with practiced precision.

"Oh God." Her voice rises, desperate. "Alessandro, I'm... I'm going to—"

"Not yet. Hold it."

"I can't, please, it's too much."

"You can. You will." My hand releases her hair, sliding around to grip her throat, not choking, just holding, owning. "You'll come when I tell you, with me buried in your ass, while I claim every last part of you. Understand?"

"Yes, sir, but please."

"Now, *tesoro*. Come for me *now*."

Permission granted, she shatters. Her entire body convulses, the orgasm ripping through her with such force she screams, a raw, primal sound, completely unrestrained. The way her body clamps down triggers my own release, spilling deep inside her while she writhes and gasps beneath me.

The pleasure is so intense that she uses her safe word "Red! Red!" Not from pain, but from the overwhelming sensation that borders on too much.

Immediately withdrawing, gathering her shaking form into my arms. "I've got you. You're safe. Breathe, *tesoro*. Just breathe."

She's trembling, tears streaming down her face, but when she looks at me, her expression is dazed satisfaction rather than distress.

"Too much?" Concern makes my voice rough.

"Perfect amount." Her laugh is shaky. "So intense. So intense I forgot how to process it."

"You did so well." Pressing kisses to her temple, her cheek, her lips. "So perfect. Took everything I gave you."

"*Yours.*" The word comes out slurred with exhaustion. "Every part of me is *yours.*"

"*Mine,*" the agreement comes fierce, possessive. "Completely *mine.*"

The care taken afterward, I clean her gently, massaging sore muscles, wrapping her in soft blankets, only makes her trust deepen visibly. She curls into me, boneless and sated, and the vulnerability in that gesture does something to my chest.

By the time exhaustion finally claims us both, she's marked everywhere. Elena has bite marks on her shoulders, fingerprints on her hips, evidence of possession written across her skin in ways that will last days. And now, having claimed her in every possible way, satisfaction runs bone-deep.

She belongs to me.

Completely.

In every way that matters.

And tomorrow, the world will learn *exactly* what that means.

"Still sure about this?" The question is murmured against her temple.

"If you ask me that one more time, I'm going to stab you." But there's no heat in the threat. "I'm sure. I've been sure. Stop questioning it."

"Can't help it. Keep waiting for you to come to your senses and run."

"Not happening." She shifts, wincing slightly.

"Though I might need a wheelchair after that. Pretty sure you've destroyed my ability to walk."

Pride and concern war in equal measure. "Too much?"

"Perfect amount." Her smile is satisfied, sated. "But Alessandro? Next time, warn me before you—"

"Before I what?"

"Before you do that thing with your..." She blushes. "Never mind. I'll just plan better."

The laugh that escapes me is genuine and warm. "Noted. Next time, I'll provide a detailed itinerary of planned activities."

"That would be helpful, yes."

We fall into comfortable silence, afternoon light filtering through the windows. Tomorrow brings challenges, Greco still lives, the Feds still investigate, enemies still circle. But right now, in this moment, peace exists. Elena is my safety, my home.

"Wait here." The bed protests as it's left, but this can't wait.

Her overnight bag yielded little when brought from the penthouse, with only a few clothes, toiletries, and a phone. But one thing was tucked in the side pocket, carefully wrapped, a single black rose, preserved somehow, with gold leaf painted along the edges of each petal.

Returning to the bedroom, I find Elena sitting up,

sheet wrapped around her, looking curious.

"What's that?"

"You sent me black roses. Three of them, to symbolize death." The preserved rose is carefully held up. "I kept one. Had it preserved and gilded. Because even in death, even in endings, something beautiful can remain."

Her eyes shine with unshed tears. "Alessandro."

"And..." The other item from the pocket comes out, a small key on a simple chain. "This is the key to my penthouse. To my home. I want you to have it. Want you to know that wherever I am, whatever I'm doing, you have a place that's yours, safe and protected."

"You're giving me a key." She says it like it's something momentous.

"I'm giving you access to my life. My space. Everything I have." The key is pressed into her palm, followed by the preserved rose. "I'm giving you my heart, Elena. In whatever form you'll accept it."

"Your heart." She looks at both items, then back at me. "Alessandro De Luca, are you asking me to move in with you?"

"I'm asking you to let me keep you safe. To share my space and my life and whatever future we can build together." The vulnerability in admitting this is new and uncomfortable. "I'm asking you to be *mine* in every way that matters. To trust me to protect you. To—"

Her kiss cuts off the rambling. When she pulls back, tears stream down her face, but her smile could light the entire city.

"Yes. To all of it, *yes*." She clutches the rose and key as though they're precious. "And Alessandro? I have something for you too."

"You do?"

"Well, not here. But..." She bites her lip. "Tomorrow is Christmas. And I may have made something for you before everything went to hell. It's at my apartment above the shop."

"Can it wait until tomorrow?"

"It should. Christmas gifts are meant for Christmas." Her smile turns impish. "Besides, the anticipation will be good for you."

"Anticipation is overrated."

"Says the man who just spent three hours edging me."

The laugh that escapes is startled. "Fair point."

She settles back into my arms, and the comfortable silence that follows is broken only by her steady breathing and the distant sounds of suburbia.

Tomorrow will bring Christmas morning in the penthouse, provided Marco arranges for her shop apartment to be cleared. Tonight, in this safe house, wrapped around each other while the world continues its violent spin, happiness feels almost possible.

Almost.

Because men like me don't get happy endings, with white picket fences and quiet retirements.

But maybe men like me get stolen moments. Get Christmas mornings with a woman who chose *us* despite everything.

Get to hold them close and pretend, just for a while, that love can triumph over violence.

Christmas morning breaks clear and cold over Seattle.

The penthouse sparkles with lights Marco's people installed overnight, a tree in the corner, garlands across the windows, stockings hung with care because apparently my second-in-command is secretly a romantic.

Elena stands at the window in one of my shirts, coffee in hand, watching the sunrise paint the city gold. She's been quiet since waking, thoughtful in a way that makes me nervous.

"Everything okay?"

"Perfect." She turns, and the smile she gives me is soft, genuine. "I was just thinking. A month ago, I was alone in my apartment, drinking coffee and wondering if I'd ever find someone who understood me. And now," She gestures at the penthouse, at me, at everything. "Now I have all this."

"Careful. That almost sounds like happiness."

"Maybe it is." She sets down her coffee and crosses to her bag, pulling out a small, wrapped package. "Merry Christmas, Alessandro."

The package is surprisingly light, wrapped in brown paper and tied with a ribbon that's definitely from her shop. Inside is a leather journal, handmade, by the looks of it, with my initials embossed in gold on the cover. The pages are thick, expensive, the kind meant for important things.

"Open it," she says softly.

The first page holds her elegant handwriting, with flowing script that must have taken hours.

For Alessandro,

Because monsters need someone to remember they're human. Because shadows need light to exist. Because every terrible thing you've done to protect what you love deserves to be balanced by something beautiful.

Write in this. Your thoughts, your fears, your hopes. The things you can't say out loud.

Let it be a place where The Shadow can rest, and Alessandro can breathe.

All my love, Elena

The subsequent pages are blank, waiting to be filled. But tucked between them are pressed flowers—white amaryllis, the same kind from the first arrangement made for my mother. Small reminders of light in a book meant to hold darkness.

"You made this." The words come out rough.

"The week before everything went to hell. I thought..." She swallows hard. "I thought maybe you needed a place that was just yours. Where you didn't have to be The Shadow or the boss or anything except yourself." Her hand covers mine. "You carry so much, Alessandro. Sometimes you need to put it down. Even if it's only on paper."

The gesture is so thoughtful, so perfectly her, that speaking becomes difficult. "It's perfect. Thank you, *tesoro*."

"You're welcome. Now..." She eyes me expectantly. "I believe it's traditional for gift exchanges to be reciprocal?"

"Greedy."

"Curious. There's a difference."

The small blue Tiffany box has been burning a hole in my pocket since collecting it yesterday. The jeweler nearly wept with joy at the commission, a custom piece, rush order, money no object.

The box is placed in her hands, and watching her face as she opens it is worth every dollar spent.

Inside, nestled in white silk, is a ring. Not a traditional engagement ring, it's too soon for that, despite how much the idea appeals. Instead, it's a cocktail ring, a large amber stone surrounded by diamonds, set in platinum. The deep honey color of the center stone matches her eyes when she's happy, and the diamonds catch the light like stars.

"Alessandro." His name is a whisper. "This is…"

"Too much?" Doubt creeps in. "I can have them change it."

"No! *God, no*. It's perfect. Absolutely perfect." She slides it onto her right hand, and it fits perfectly because, of course, Marco got her ring size somehow. "But this must have cost—"

"Don't worry about cost. Worry about whether you like it."

"I *love* it." She holds her hand up, watching the stones catch the light. "But Alessandro, this is significant. Rings mean something."

"Yes, they do." Taking her hand, I study the ring, her hand in mine, the stone glinting between us.

"They mean you're *mine*. I'm claiming you publicly. Anyone who looks at you will know you belong to The Shadow."

"Possessive."

"Extremely." No point in denying it. "But Elena, this isn't just about possession. It's about—" *How to explain what she means?* "It's about the fact that you're the best thing to happen to me in fifteen years. You see the monster and choose to stay anyway. You make me want to be better than I am, even though I'll probably fail spectacularly."

"You won't fail."

"You don't know that."

"I do. Because I'll be there to remind you." She rises on her toes, kissing me softly. "We'll figure it out together. The monster and the florist. The Shadow and the light. All of it."

"*Together*," the word is tested, tasted. "I like the sound of that."

"Good. Because you're stuck with me now." She glances at the clock. "Though speaking of stuck, don't you have a crime empire to run? Enemies to vanquish? Federal investigations to dodge?"

"All of that can wait." I wrap my arms around her waist, pulling her close. "Today is Christmas. Today, I'm just Alessandro, and you're just Elena, and nothing else matters."

"Just Alessandro and just Elena," she repeats, smiling. "I like that too."

"Good. Because tomorrow, reality returns. Tomorrow, we deal with Greco and the Feds and everything else." The promise comes dark, certain. "But today, today is ours."

"Ours," she agrees, settling into my arms. "The perfect Christmas."

"Not quite perfect yet. But it will be." The words come quietly, meant for me as much as her. "Soon, you'll legally belong to me. Soon, everyone will know that Elena Harper is under The Shadow's protection. And, *tesoro*…" The ring catches the light as her hand rests over my heart. "Soon, you'll be Elena De Luca. My wife. My heart. *Mine* in every way the law and God and this violent world recognize."

She looks up, eyes wide. "Are you, is that—"

"Not a proposal. Not yet." Though the hunger for it burns. "But a promise. When this mess with Greco is settled, when the immediate danger passes, I'm going to ask you properly. On my knees if it's what you want. With a ring that makes this one look like a placeholder."

"I don't need a bigger ring."

"But you'll get one anyway, because you deserve everything I can give you." The kiss is soft, reverent. "You deserve a man who's worthy of you, but you're stuck with me instead. I'm going to spend the rest of my life making sure you never regret this choice."

"I could never regret choosing you."

"You say that now. Wait until you've survived a

few years of my world."

"Then I guess we'll find out together." Her smile is pure sunshine. "Merry Christmas, Alessandro."

"Merry Christmas, *tesoro*."

And standing there in the penthouse with city lights sparkling and a woman who chose darkness wrapped in my arms, happiness doesn't feel quite so impossible anymore.

Still unlikely.

Still probably doomed.

But *possible*.

And for a man like me, possibility is more than enough.

THE END

Want to find out what happens to
Alessandro and Elena?
https://dl.bookfunnel.com/h9uyijub8j
for your Bonus Content

Have you read:

Tackling Love

https://books2read.com/u/bPoYVl

Colton Anders.

Quarterback for the New England Warriors.
Playboy, cocky, self-assured, used to getting what
he wants.

Skye Hadley.

Teacher at a high-profile private school.
Quiet, plays it safe, dedicated employee.
Unexpectedly, their worlds collide.
Colton tempts Skye, and she throws caution to the

wind and takes him home.
Unknowingly propelling herself into a world filled
with fans, media and lots of attention.

The media attention is grueling, but the chemistry
is undeniable. Vulnerable in lust, Skye wants
nothing more than to give in to her heart's desires.

*With the world watching will Colt be able to win
Skye over in this fun, sports romance?*

Tackling Life

https://books2read.com/u/4XWqJN

Grayson Moore linebacker for the
New England Warriors.

His whole life has been working up to this
moment, the moment when his team
wins the Superbowl.
But life has a way of throwing you an illegal pass.

Diandra Evergrow was the love of his life,
well, until she ended it.
Now she's walked back in, on the best night of his
life with news that could destroy not only him but

all those that are close to him.

Will Grayson put it all on the line for the
woman that once claimed his heart?
Or will he tuck and run to protect it?

Property of Blade

https://readerlinks.com/l/4251862

Blade

Alaska is my kingdom, and as President of the Kings of Anarchy, I keep control of my men and secrets that could tear our lives apart

Life here is simple—no one asks questions, and I don't offer answers.

But when I find Hannah stranded and out of her depth, everything shifts. She doesn't belong in my world, yet I can't stop thinking about her.

Hannah

I came here to escape my life in Los Angeles. A fresh start away from friends, family, and him. After my accident, he left me because I wasn't "perfect" anymore. For over a year, I tried to make it work, but every time he looked at me, I saw the revulsion in his eyes.

So, I sold everything I owned, packed up my cat, Grace, and moved to one of the remotest places I could find—Alaska.

Can Hannah accept the beast inside Blade and the broken men he leads, or will the brutal truth of their worlds rip them apart?

Get ready for a raw, gritty ride through Alaska's wild terrain, where danger lurks at every turn, and love is anything but easy in *Property of Blade, Kings of Anarchy MC Alaska.*

Property of Vex
https://readerlinks.com/l/4627380

Property of Prophet
https://books2read.com/u/mZol52
Available September 2026
Preorder NOW!

Kathleen Kelly

The Savage Angels MC Series

Savage Stalker Book 1
The Savage Angels MC Series

BLURB

Dane Reynolds
President of the Savage Angels MC.
Fierce, strong, and loyal.
He's had his eye on Kat for a while now and has
been waiting for her to come to him, but he's had
enough of waiting.
He's decided it's time to make her his.

Katarina Saunders
Kat to the world, international rock star.
Lead singer for The Grinders.
Until she has an accident that ruins her career and
sends her running into the mountains, away from
everything and everyone.
Will these two come together?

Or will Kat's *savage stalker* get to her first?

From *USA Today* Bestselling Author Kathleen Kelly.

A Merry Little Vendetta

Savage Fire Book 2
Savage Town Book 3
Savage Lover Book 4
Savage Sacrifice Book 5
Savage Rebel (Novella) Book 6
Savage Lies Book 7
Savage Life Book 8
Savage Christmas (Novella) Book 9
Savage Release Book 10
Savage Heart Book 11
Savage Angels Book 12
Savage Angels MC Collection Books 1-9

MacKenny Brothers Series
An MC/Band of Brothers Romance

Spark
Spark of Vengeance
Spark of Hope
Spark of Deception
Spark of Time
Spark of Redemption
Spark of Passion

Kathleen Kelly

Wraith Novels
Wraith
Fealty: A Wraith Novel
Wraith Boxset
Includes: Wraith, Fealty and Shadow which is only
available in this boxset.

Standalones

Cardinal: The Affinity Chronicles Book One
Snake's Revenge: Gritty Devils MC
The Secrets We Hold

Hey there, lovely reader!
Thanks a million for grabbing this book - you rock!
Now, I'm not above a little shameless begging…
Pretty please, with a cherry on top,
leave a review wherever you picked this up.
Your thoughts help other readers discover
My wild and wonderful world of
romance and mayhem.
Plus, you'll earn major karma points!
Thank you for supporting indie authors like me.
Stay awesome!

Connect With ME ONLINE

Check these links for more from
Kathleen Kelly

READER GROUP

Want access to fun, prizes and sneak peeks?
Join my Facebook Reader Group.
https://bit.ly/32X17pv

NEWSLETTER

Want to see what's next?
Sign up for my Newsletter.
https://www.subscribepage.com/kathleenkellyauthor

BOOKBUB

Connect with me on Bookbub.
https://www.bookbub.com/authors/kathleen-kelly

A Merry Little Vendetta

GOODREADS

Add my books to your TBR list
on my Goodreads profile.
http://bit.ly/1xsOGxk

AMAZON

Buy my books from my Amazon profile.
https://amzn.to/2JCUT6q

WEBSITE

https://kathleenkellyauthor.com/

TWITTER

https://twitter.com/kkellyauthor

INSTAGRAM

https://instagram.com/kathleenkellyauthor

EMAIL

kathleenkellyauthor@gmail.com

FACEBOOK

https://bit.ly/36jlaQV

AUTHOR

Kathleen Kelly, a USA Today Best-Selling Author and an International Best-Selling Author, is known for her fast-paced, spicy romance novels. Kathleen writes MC, Paranormal, Sports, and Band of Brothers Romance.

When she's not writing, she's collecting handbags (they always fit!) and planning her next international trip.

Kathleen can be spotted in local cafes, blending in with the regulars while plotting her next tale of passion and intrigue. She finds inspiration in the quirky characters around her, real and fictional alike.

Living in Toowoomba, Queensland, with her childhood sweetheart, SL, rescue sweetheart Freya, and Eir, the soon-to-be gigantic Maine Coon who thinks she's the main character, Kathleen values kindness, loyalty, and good stories.

If you have any questions about her novels or would like to ask Kathleen a question, she can be contacted via e-mail:

kathleenkellyauthor@gmail.com

or she can be found on Facebook. Kathleen welcomes messages from readers who share her love for stories that leave hearts racing and cheeks blushing.